UNSHAKABLE

Patricia Snelling

Published in New Zealand by Inthelight Publishers

Bible scriptures have been taken from the World English Bible (WEB)

First printed as Rescue Net in 2017
Republished as Unshakable in 2019

National Library of New Zealand Catalogue

Website: www.patriciasnelling.com
https://www.facebook.com/PatriciaSnellingAuthor

Harold Joyce Cover Art
Martin Joyce Graphic Design
Judith White Literary Assistance

Other Books by Author:

When Hope Went South (Dart River Series)
Missing On Kawau
Broken Web

Chapter One

At Auckland International Airport, Ruby rummaged through her hand luggage for her electronic tickets. She'd forgotten to put them in with her passport in the belt bag where she could easily grab them.

'We have to be at Departures over there. You can drop me off at the front door so I can get checked in.' Ruby glanced at her watch and bit down hard on her lip.

As she dragged her luggage to the check-in counter, she continually checked her watch. Fortunately, the queue was moving fast.

Cherie, her mother gently tugged on her arm. 'We've got a few minutes. Let's go for a coffee.'

Lyon, her adoptive father led the way to an airport café. Ruby slowly sipped on an iced coffee and saw the colour had drained from her mother's cheeks. Cherie's face looked like a porcelain doll, revealing deep shadows under her eyes. Ruby knew her mother was reluctant to see her daughter travel alone.

'I'll be back, Mum, honest—and you and Dad have been travelling backwards and forwards to Thailand so you need to give me the chance to travel too.'

Cherie looked up and gave her a half-smile. 'I know dear. I'm just a normal Mum who clucks over her children. You could have flown directly to Bangkok instead of travelling overland with Kate. It would be much safer.'

Just then her flight was announced over the intercom.

'Qantas flight YPA5QH to Sydney proceed to Gate 28.'

Ruby's stomach churned. Remnants of the cream topped iced coffee she'd consumed formed whirlpools in her throat.

'Mum— sorry, I'll have to go. That's my flight! I'll phone you when I arrive. Don't worry, I've done this before, remember?'

'I know, but not overland through Asia— be careful, Ruby.'

She gave them both a hug and took off along the lengthy corridor—a woman on a mission with fire in her belly.

***

During the flight, Ruby pulled a letter out from her handbag, the most recent one she'd received from her friend, Kate and re-read it. Kate had told her that she'd been feeling a lack of purpose in her life. She'd also confided that she'd become ambivalent towards her spiritual life and needed direction. Ruby had replied to the letter inviting Kate to travel with her to Thailand to visit her parent's charity—a safe house for children, victims of sex trafficking. Her parents had originally financed the residence called Rainbow Haven run by the organisation Rescue Net with their own money until sufficient funding came. Now Ruby was hungry for adventure, a risky one her parents had warned.

Kate was waiting for Ruby at Sydney airport, smiling from ear to ear. 'So good to see you girl, it's been ages. You're looking so well.' Ruby couldn't keep her eyes off Kate's trendy summer outfit.

'And you've lost weight you lucky thing. That's good because I've got a big lunch waiting for you back at the flat.' Kate sped off, almost side-swiping a car that lurched sideways. She continued. 'I hope you like ham and asparagus quiche with parmesan.'

Ruby felt uneasy with Kate's driving, but not enough to lose her appetite. 'I'm so hungry I could eat a horse. They starve you on those flights— I like the car, is this a VDub? You didn't have this last time I was here!'

'Mum and Dad bought it for me when I passed my Masters. It was a surprise.'

Ruby knew Kate's parents were well off, and although she tried hard not to compare herself with others, she felt a hint of envy. As she sat waiting for her to dish up lunch, her eyes scanned the expensive looking furniture and décor.

'If you feel up to it, I could show you a tentative itinerary I've put together for our overland trip.'

'Sounds great, I'm keen to get it sorted too. The only thing is we won't be able to go through the Middle East. There's too much conflict there at present.'

'You said in your letter you wanted to stay on in Thailand for a while to help out at Rescue Net. I'll just fly directly to London from there,' said Kate.

'That's why we both need to sit down and put together a plan. Let's do it as soon as possible.'

The next morning they completed planning their itinerary then walked into the small shopping mall to the travel agent. The woman at the desk handed them a printout of ticket prices.

As they wandered along the promenade Ruby spotted a gelato ice-cream parlour. 'Oh boy, real gelato. Just look at all the flavours!' She peered through the window. 'I just love the stuff. I haven't had one for ages.'

They both walked out of the shop with a large waffle cone of gelato each.

'Let's go sit on that wall over there.' Kate pointed towards the beach.

'How are your parents going Ruby? Are they still at that retreat in the Bay Of Plenty? Cromwell Mead isn't it?'

'Yes, they're still there. In fact, they purchased it from the managers, Anne and Murray. They've had to spend some time at Rescue Net in Thailand— but most of the time they have locals running the Safe Houses now as they have it well set up. They just oversee it mostly from a distance.'

***

The overnight train to Kyogle chugged into the station. The girls motored along the platform to catch it with rucksacks and sunhats flying.

'Hurry Ruby, we don't want to miss it— they only run once a day!'

The train from Sydney was half empty, and to their delight so was their carriage, except for an elderly couple and a young family. They were on the way to Ruby's friend Jane in Bonalbo, New South Wales. She said she would be sending a friend to collect them from Kyogle Station.

They slept until early morning. The sun was like a ball of flame as it woke Ruby. As she stared out the window to look at the wildlife, her mouth dropped wide open when she caught sight of the giant Kangaroos that jumped alongside the train. It was as though they were competing in a race with the train. She especially noticed the one with the cute baby Joey in its pouch and quickly captured the photos on her digital camera.

'Howdy girls— where do you hail from? I detect a strange accent.' Two local ranchers wearing leather western hats slithered into the seat in front of them.

'Oh no. Here we go', Ruby muttered to herself.

'We're visiting a friend in Bonalbo,' said Kate. 'We come from Auckland, New Zealand.'

The men had never left New South Wales Ruby thought. They may as well have said Timbuktu. One of the men couldn't stop talking and showing off. 'We're from Charbray Cattle Station near Bonalbo. We'll be getting off first.'

4

And thank goodness you try-hards. Ruby squeezed her nose. 'Ooh, they stank of horse hair,' she cried.

She pressed her face up against the window, determined to see some more wildlife, especially a koala bear. Before long, the train chugged its way around a corner towards Kyogle. It slowed as it approached the station about a kilometre from the platform. As it went through a thicket of tall trees, Ruby looked up at the towering Gum trees. Then she could hardly believe what she saw. Brown cuddly looking things like soft toys, most of them lying on their backs sound asleep or curled up around a branch. She elbowed Kate. 'Quick, look up there—Koala Bears!'

Ruby hurriedly tried to take some photos but was not quick enough. This is what she'd come all this way for. But just seeing the animals so close by, made her feel triumphant.

When they finally arrived in Kyogle, Ruby experienced some travel fatigue and complained to Kate.

'You'd better harden up girl, especially for travelling later overland through South East Asia,' said Kate, acting in a domineering manner sounding like an intrepid traveller.

'I just couldn't get to sleep at your flat. I can't take road noise and this wasn't exactly a comfortable train ride either.'

Chapter Two

Merv waved at them as they disembarked from the train at Kyogle. They were the only ones getting off.

'Hi girls, Merv's the name. Welcome to the New South Wales outback. Jane sent me to collect you.'

'Hi Merv, thanks for coming. Jane wrote and described what you look like.' Ruby grinned, her eyes squinting in the harsh Australian sun. She dug around in her bag for her sunglasses.

Merv appeared amused. 'I hope she said to look out for a tall handsome dude.' They all laughed.

'Come on, girls— there's plenty of room in the front of my Ute. Climb in. I'll throw your bags in the back with Blue, my working dog.'

Ruby peered at the dog before she climbed in. She noticed its intense blue eyes. It appeared friendly. Merv called it an Australian Shepherd, a breed she hadn't seen before.

She elbowed Kate to climb in, but Kate pushed Ruby in first. Ruby felt uncomfortable brushing up against a perfect stranger, especially in such an intimate position.

Merv wanted to talk and find out all about them.

'What brings you here? Are you on holiday?'

After Kate elaborated on their academic achievements and qualifications, she told him about their plans to travel overland to Thailand and her own plans to carry on to London.

'Well, you sure are a gutsy pair. That trip is not for the faint-hearted I hear. Have some mates who have done it.'

'Do you work on one of the big cattle stations around here?' Ruby found her tongue.

'I'm the local vet. I've been in this area all my life— same as Jane. She's teaching at the local school and I know her family really well. Her sister works as a remote nurse, but she's home on holiday right now. Her mother's a widow. How do you know Jane?' He nodded at Ruby.

'I met her on a bus tour back home. We were touring the lakes down south. She was on the tour with her sister Maggie.'

When they arrived in Bonalbo, Jane and her mother rushed out to meet them. Ruby and Jane couldn't wait to be alone to share their news.

'Why don't you stay for dinner Merv? Just to say thanks for picking up the girls,' said Jane's mother. 'After you girls have settled in, perhaps you could all go for walk.'

'Hey, you two— let me show you the schoolhouse before dinner and we can all catch up.' Jane lifted her hand to point them in the direction of the school across the road. 'Merv said he'll help Mum with the roast.'

Jane was acting very proud of the way she'd built up the schoolhouse into something worthwhile. The roll only had twenty pupils but it was growing. She strutted around like a peacock, with an air of importance.

'Hey, girls—what do you think of Merv? He's still an eligible bachelor.'

'We thought you were tied up with him, Jane. He seems to know all about you from his conversation during the trip here.' Why was Jane being elusive about him? Ruby wondered.

'No, really, we're just good friends and he's not interested in anything else. We went to school together. There's nothing going on.'

Kate didn't let on, but the way she'd looked him up and down back at the house had made it obvious to Ruby that she'd found him rather cute.

The girls sat down, eager to have a catch up about how their lives had been going.

At dinner that evening, Jane made sure she placed Kate at the table next to Merv. She must have picked up the vibes too, thought Ruby.

The next day Merv showed them around his vet clinic. Ruby could see he was attracted to Kate by the way he kept walking next to her and his whirlpool brown eyes never left Kate's face. Ruby felt a bit left out. But she could see her friend with someone like him in the future, as she knew Kate well.

'So, can I convince you to become a veterinary nurse, Kate? I can sure do with an assistant here and none of the nurses want to leave the city to come and work here in such a remote community.'

Kate laughed and acted dismissively towards him to hide her embarrassment, although she appeared to like the attention he gave her.

***

Jane's mother drove the girls all the way to Brisbane. She wanted to visit relatives there and offered to drop them off at the backpackers in the city.

As she drove onto the highway, Jane took Kate by surprise. 'Kate, it appears you turned Merv's head while you were in Bonalbo. He asked me to see if you would give him a forwarding address in Thailand. He would like to write to you.'

'Oh, why is that?' Kate's face turned pink.

'He thought you'd both struck a chord in some way.'

'Well, I suppose we did hit it off quite well. But what's the point to all this anyway? He lives so far away and I'm off to London after we arrive in Thailand.'

'He wants to keep in touch. Perhaps he hopes you might come back to Bonalbo and spend a bit longer in the area.'

Kate wrote down her details. 'I doubt anything will come of this. We live too far away from each other.'

Kate and Ruby had been looking forward to this big overseas experience called the Big OE. They had both been stressed studying their Masters and working full time. Kate had completed her Nursing Masters and Ruby a Degree in Social Work. It was time for a break.

Ruby had grown up with a basic faith in God with her parents being Christians but had not felt any passionate purpose or God's direction in her life. She felt as though she didn't really know who she was, lacking a form of self-identity.

Kate was in a similar state. Both young girls had been regular members of the University Christian Fellowship. Kate had become quite worldly since Ruby saw her last.

At the backpackers, Ruby unrolled her sleeping bag and prepared her bed for the night. She took out a packet of dark chocolate, broke off a piece, and handed it to Kate. 'Here ... our dessert.'

'Thanks! Hey Ruby— what happened to that guy Richard you were engaged to, did he get in touch again? He was working as a doctor somewhere overseas, wasn't he?'

'No ... it took me a long time to get over that. He suddenly dumped me when he was offered a post-graduate position in Brazil and wouldn't wait for me to finish my Social Work degree.'

'Did he not ask you to go with him?'

'He asked my mother if it was okay to take me to Brazil. She told him it wasn't safe, as I was too young. She was concerned that if we broke up, I'd be stranded there.'

'So he just up and left you?'

'He tried to put the blame on my mother, but he just didn't want to wait another year.'

'Did he keep writing to you from there?'

'All that time, the only things he sent were impersonal postcards about the weather. Whereas his mother had received long letters with all his news. That hurt me deeply.' Her voice quavered.

'Did you ever see him again?'

Ruby wanted to tell Kate to stop badgering her with sensitive questions but held back.

'When I had finished my Degree he appeared on my doorstep but I was involved with someone else. He had been visiting his folks and asked if I'd go back to Brazil with him. He had offered to pay for my ticket but I told him I wasn't interested.'

'Why was that? I thought you loved him.'

Ruby's eyes glazed over. 'I realised he didn't genuinely love me. It would have just been a marriage of convenience for him.'

Ruby suddenly felt overwhelmed with tiredness— or was it unresolved grief that weighed her down. Perhaps it was that she was feeling angry rather than fragile. She had been abandoned and her trust in men had been damaged. Richard was her first love, and she'd been crazy about him. Things were so different now.

***

The flight from Brisbane to Cairns took three hours. They were able to hire a caravan in a tourist park for a good price

10

instead of being stuck in a girls' dorm in a busy backpackers. Ruby valued the quietness.

They found the pool at the Tourist Park. The swim in the clear blue water was a welcome treat after all the travelling.

Ruby stood wringing out her long hair with her large beach towel. Then she wrapped a tropical sarong around her waist.

'Have you seen where the laundry is yet Kate? I want to wear this top and it's looking pretty grubby. I need to give it a rinse out.'

'It's around the back somewhere. I saw the sign.'

They sat with their coffee by the pool, doing some more reminiscing about their first year at university when they had become close friends. They talked until the sun went down.

***

They both had some part-time work in Cairns for a few weeks. Ruby worked for a shuttle company. She drove beach buggies to the airport to collect tourists and drove them to their hotels. The highlight was feeling the wind in her face and the sun on her shoulders as she sped down the highways. It was exhilarating. The Americans gave her generous tips, which was a real bonus, as the job did not pay well.

Kate was offered work through her father's friend who owned a large company in Cairns. He needed someone to vacuum his huge swimming pool once a week for a good wage. She also worked as a Postie part-time riding a bicycle which she hoped would help her stay trim.

'Oh boy, I'm bushed. My legs are killing me from all that biking.' This time it was Kate who was doing the complaining. Two months of delivering mail by bicycle had got to her. She wasn't as fit as she thought she was.

Relieved that their working stint had come to an end, the two girls sat calculating the funds they had for their trip. Ruby picked up the travel guide called "Across Asia on the Cheap". 'We could take a bus to Darwin but it would take days and there's not much to see on the way. I think we should fly.' she felt she would die of boredom sitting for days on a bus.

'There's a good deal going at the moment, but we have to leave early next Tuesday.'

Ruby started to feel elated at the thought of getting closer to leaving Australia. Their great adventure was about to begin. Even the thought of staying in tropical Darwin intrigued her. Especially meeting some of the Aboriginals in the outback. She loved people, especially learning about those from different cultures and backgrounds.

The next morning they set off on their four-hour flight to Darwin with a little more money in their bank accounts to fund their adventure.

As they walked out of Darwin airport, they walked into a wall of damp, humid heat. Ruby found it difficult to breathe momentarily.

'Don't worry Ruby the humidity will be good for your asthma— honestly.' Kate's tone sounded unconvincing.

Ruby was only mild asthmatic but the dense Australian flora in Cairns had triggered a few episodes and she had used her inhaler.

The tiny cabin they were offered was cramped, but it had a flush toilet. For the rest, they had to use the camp communal kitchen and shower block. At least there was a large swimming pool near their cabin.

Early the next morning, Ruby took a hot shower in the ablution block. After dressing, she took her time applying sunblock lotion. She thought she heard men's voices, loud ones at that, somewhere outside. Perhaps it was in the male shower block next door.

As she walked outside, she could hear the commotion was coming from the park reserve over the fence. She could see two men on the ground. They were Aboriginal men lying on the grass under a large tree.

'Get up you black bastard, you know this place is out of bounds for you lot! We need to teach you a few manners!'

The two men appeared confused and disorientated as if drunk. The policemen dragged them roughly to their feet. The officers then brutalised them with batons and literally threw them into the back of the van.

Ruby's head spun with outrage. She felt a vein in her neck throb. She couldn't believe her eyes and never knew that this sort of thing happened in Australia. She'd read all about South Africa and how the black South Africans were treated during Apartheid.

She ran back to the cabin, trying to decide what to do about it. She couldn't exactly go to the police station to lay a complaint against the police. How can humans treat others so cruelly without an ounce of feeling or remorse? How had she been so naïve all her life?

Chapter Three

'Ruby—what's happened? You look like you've seen a ghost!'

'I wish I had ... It would have been a lot better than what I've just seen!' She made herself a coffee and sat on her bed, telling Kate about the outrageous horrific scene she'd just witnessed.

'I remember reading articles about this sort of thing happening over here.' Kate attempted to offer Ruby support, as she became aware that she'd been badly affected by the incident.

'But the police are supposed to keep us safe from violence, not inflict it!' Ruby's voice started wavering. 'I had to do some research on human rights and ethnic brutality for my Master's degree. I've read some pretty sobering articles about police violence, but in America, not Australia.'

'There's not a lot one can do about it, except send articles to the newspaper and see if they'll do an editorial on it. The police will only deny it if you report them to higher authorities,' Kate replied.

Ruby struggled to sleep that night. She couldn't get the image out of her mind, feeling great empathy for the victims in the park and what their fate would be. To add insult to injury later that week, she read reports of Aboriginal prison inmates committing suicide. She was enraged at the inequality of life.

'Come on Ruby, cheer up! Let's go out and grab some food. It'll give us a lift.'

There were people from various countries and ethnicities staying in the tourist park. Kate and Ruby became friendly with a few people their own ages. There were two young men in the camp from Auckland University. They'd been travelling in a campervan and were about to fly out to Timor too.

Rick, an Englishman, was an Engineer with the Royal Marines, and Jamie, from Auckland, had qualified as a Physiotherapist and had been working in London. They were close friends. The girls both realised they had seen Jamie around at the University Christian Fellowship meetings. He was popular and Ruby knew he had a good reputation.

'Hey girls, why don't you join us? We are just firing up the barbeque.' Rick appeared to be overconfident, the forward one.

'What do you think, Ruby, do you want to?' Kate asked, nudging her firmly in the ribs.

'I suppose we could share a meal with them.'

'Okay,' Kate called, 'We'll bring a salad.'

They all seemed to get on quite well but the girls both found Rick to be loud and egotistical. They discussed travelling together as a group as far as Thailand.

'Well, that's settled. We'll all travel together and split up in Bangkok. We have our tickets booked for next Wednesday if you two can get on that flight. Otherwise, we can wait for you at Bacau Backpackers until you arrive.' Jamie appeared to be trying to take the initiative.

The girls managed to get on the same flights as the men, heading for Bacau, East Timor. As they left the travel agent, they discussed their decision to join up with the men in Timor.

'I guess it would be safer travelling in those countries with some males in tow. What do you think, Ruby?' Kate sat at the breakfast table, piling the butter on her toast. She licked her fingers.

'As long as they behave themselves. I don't want any trouble. I'm not so sure about Rick, he's a bit of a try hard, but Jamie seems like a respectable sort of bloke. If they give us any grief, we can leave them there.'

Ruby thought they were being too trusting, and she was even more aware of her lack of experience in these situations, being shy by nature. Was she making the right decision to travel with these men?

She was looking forward to travelling overland to her parent's charity in Thailand.

'Timor is quite primitive and pretty rough in places, I hear. It may be in our best interests to travel with the men as chaperones until we get to Bangkok.' Kate was making sure Ruby was not going to back out.

'I have a travel guide that says that we need to keep our valuables close as a lot of stealing that goes on there.' Ruby waved it in front of Kate's nose.

'That's why we need to keep anything valuable, including passports in our belt bags.' Kate spoke indignantly.

'I'm dreading that long journey between Dili and Kupang. I'm glad we get a few breaks on the way.'

To Ruby's delight, the flight took less than two hours. Rick and Jamie were waiting for them in the arrival lounge. Both the girls were relieved to find they could get on the same flight as the men.

'Let's head for that beach Osolata we've been told about.' Kate seemed to want to take charge.

'That's right ... that's where most people stay here on the cheap,' Ruby said, hoping they could sleep outdoors under the stars.' She closed her travel guide and followed Kate over to the carousel to collect their baggage.

'Hurry up all of you, the bus leaves for Osolata beach in ten minutes, and we've got a little way to walk to get it.

Otherwise, we'll have to stay in town tonight.' Rick puffed out his chest, stiffening his jaw.

They sat in the bus staring out at the view from the windows. Miles of pristine white sand and azure blue sea.

'I hope the driver knows where to drop us. And it's all uphill on the way back, all five miles of it.' Rick was trying to wind the girls up. 'I'll check with the driver to see when the bus will be passing this way again tomorrow.'

Ruby sat in the front next to the driver. She'd learned a little Indonesian but her accent made it almost impossible for him to understand her.

'Why don't we set up camp first before we eat?' Kate started unrolling her blanket before spreading out her sleeping bag. 'The heat is killing me here— let's move under a tree over there.'

It was a beautiful clear night sky and the silence so profound that one could hear a pin drop. Except for the occasional sound of a small animal scuttering around in the darkness. Ruby found it unnerving.

Kate confessed, 'We must be nuts doing this. We wouldn't need to let our imaginations run wild here.' Her voice sounded croaky.

They slept soundly, lulled to sleep by the gentle waves. The humid heat had been draining and the refreshing tropical sea air revived them.

Next morning, the four of them were awakened early by the bright sunlight and heat. They were all ravenous.

'Man, I could do with a good feed of bacon and eggs right now— I'm famished.' Rick had already pulled out his compact gas cooker and opened a can of baked beans.

'I was talking to a bloke at the beach who said we can get a bus across the border after we present our visa and passport there. We can continue on the bus to Kupang and stop at various points of interest on the way.' Jamie expounded sounding well informed.

'Let's go and see some of the waterfalls and the amazing untouched white sandy beaches so talked about,' Ruby said, wide-eyed.

***

Back in Bacau, they made inquiries about how to get to Dili. Jamie had been doing his own research on the cheapest way to get there, considering their options were limited.

'There's an old barge that goes to Dili tomorrow morning. It may not be too comfortable—packed with locals fighting for a seat. But it's the quickest way to get there and by far the cheapest.' He pulled out several cans of Coca Cola from his rucksack and handed them around.

Ruby wondered why Jamie was so generous compared to Rick. He appeared to be more interested in the common welfare of the group. A quality which was far removed from his friend.

Their two-night stay in Dili was enough for them. They wanted to get away from the commercial aspect of Timor and escape to the great outdoors.

The boat trip was not too rough and was shorter than they expected. Ruby found the warm breeze inviting after the sticky, suffocating humidity of the primitive backpackers.

As they walked along the beach, they noticed a group of locals standing around a concrete trough. A young English couple were bathing their toddler in cold water using a tap next to the trough. The water was from a bore. The Timorese people couldn't take their eyes off the toddler who had white hair and blue eyes. It was as if they saw him as a kind of god.

'This is the shed they used to call the Hippie Hilton years ago, isn't it?' Kate looked intrigued at the humble looking shed with a straw roof.

They were so relieved to find fresh running water, though Ruby wondered if it was a precious commodity and questioned whether it should be used for bathing the child. Especially when the sea was available for washing.

They spoke to some of the young people who had travelled up the island from Kupang. They gave them some good pointers to put towards a workable plan they could all agree to.

'We can get a lift to the beach at Atapupu with one of the local drivers. He accepts a few American dollars to travel in his minibus,' Rick spouted, strutting around with a beach towel around him, showing off his torso to the girls.

'Then what do we do there? We aren't going to be stranded I hope.' Kate's eyebrows knitted together in a frown. Rick ignored her.

'I hope you girls have some strong hiking boots. If any of the vehicles break down on these rough roads, we may have to walk for miles.' Jamie always made the girls aware of the pitfalls of travelling in such remote locations.

'Don't worry— that's what we're here for. We do have our uses you realise.' Rick's male chauvinism irritated Ruby.

The three-hour journey on a long, bumpy, and dusty road with the local man called Ario was arduous, coupled with the friendly fellow's compulsive chatting. They paid him and included a generous tip. He beamed from ear to ear. He said he would be in Atambua about five o'clock the next day if they wanted a lift further down the island and would meet them at the backpackers.

They decided they would hike from Atapupu beach to Atambua, seventeen kilometres after the border crossing at Batugade. For Rick this was nothing, being a tough Marine, but for the girls, it was a huge challenge. Though they didn't want to let on to him.

Both the men and the girls had small gas cookers and prepared modest meals with their dried food and rice. Rick had packed some dried meat called Bilton, which he reluctantly shared.

They relished the pristine, white sandy beach and pure, clear water. It was idyllic. After their meal and a rest, they splashed around in the sea like frisky school children and the water was as warm as a heated pool. This was the life for Ruby, a little touch of paradise on earth and she didn't want it to end. It was almost perfect, except for a certain travelling companion they were stuck with.

It was a clear warm night. The stars were like sparkling diamonds.

'Look! There goes another shooting star. There are so many of them,' Kate yelled with amazement.

'Not really, it's just that we don't really notice them living in the city because of all the artificial lights and smog.' Jamie leaned over and poked the fire with a stick.

They stretched out their sleeping bags on the beach and fell asleep. Before Ruby had slowly drifted off, she was thinking about their trip so far. She and Kate were fortunate to have the lads travelling with them. She convinced herself that at least the men hadn't tried any funny business and were reasonably respectful towards the girls.

They were woken by the bright sunlight again and the rhythmic lapping of waves against the sand. The men were hungry, already tucking into their breakfast cereals with powdered milk and water from their spare canteen. The girls followed suit.

Chapter Four

The long walk to Atambua was unrelentingly tiring in the intense heat of the sun. The girls regretted agreeing to it but did not let on.

'I'm glad I've some decent hiking boots with all this walking we're having to do,' Kate whined.

They'd walked about ten kilometres and came to a river crossing. The make-shift bridge had been washed away as there had been a storm before they arrive. Some vehicles were parked alongside the road. Jamie went to talk to one of the locals to find out what was going on.

'Sorry girls. We'll have to wade through the river. There will be a truck on the other side that'll give us a lift to Atambua if we pay them something.'

Ruby felt disenchanted with the idea and Kate tried to act bravely. 'I suppose it's better than having to walk another seven or eight kilometres. My feet are killing me!'

'Right— who's going first?' Rick stood with a cocksure expression on his face.

'I think you should. You sound so confident, Rick.' Kate could barely hide her resentment.

'Rick, I think that you and I should carry the girls' rucksacks in front of us so they can be hands-free. The rocks are very slippery and it's thigh deep.' Jamie was acting like a gentleman as usual.

'Sure, I don't mind, but we'd better have a cigarette lighter ready as we'll need one to kill the leeches,' he muttered triumphantly.

'What, Leeches? No one said anything about leeches in the rivers!' Ruby wanted to make a run for it.

'I just remembered. Don't worry. I'll kill them before they have time to suck your blood to death.' Rick produced a lighter as though he had already rehearsed the scenario.

The men followed the girls close behind into the dirty, muddy river, carrying their rucksacks.

At one point Ruby almost fell over when she slipped on a rock.

'Ah— help! Get these filthy things off me. Quick, Rick!' Kate screamed, panicking, trying to brush the leeches of her legs.

'Don't do that! They won't come off that way.' Rick approached her with a lighter to burn them off, smirking.

'They are on me too. Quick— over here,' Ruby yelled.

'You'll probably bleed for a while. They inject an anti-coagulant into your skin, but the bleeding will stop', said Rick.

'You'll need to wash the wounds when we get to the river bank and apply some antiseptic.' Jamie added, hastening everyone on to the other side.

They were almost on the other side of the river, just a metre, or two from the water's edge when Ruby screamed, 'Help! Quick, run, a snake's coming after me!' They all stood and watched as Ruby raced out of the water chased by a water snake. It appeared like a lightning flash then in a split second it disappeared. Poor Ruby shook all over.

'Are you alright, Ruby? Did it bite you?' Kate was concerned for her friend.

'No, it just startled me as it just came out from nowhere.'

'What a horrible place the tropics are. So many creepy crawlies everywhere. I don't know how the locals cope with it all.' Kate started losing more and more interest in this great overseas adventure.

They stood on the river bank, relieved to be away from the hidden dangers of the murky water. Kate bent down to help

Ruby wash the blood off her legs and apply iodine. She and the men did the same as they all had a few bites which were painless but bleeding.

Though the men had been bitten, they did not dare show any weakness in front of the girls. The girls were grateful they were there to deal with the creatures.

Ruby knew that she and Kate wouldn't have coped without them coming to the rescue. In fact, they wouldn't have done this overland thing on their own, not in this sort of territory. They would have discovered that early in their travels and probably have just taken a flight directly to Thailand.

As they made their way down the poorly marked, dusty road, the girls both agreed that they both had made a mistake letting the men talk them into hiking along the boring route from Atapupu to Atambua.

They knew that a bus usually travelled through twice a day, but due to rough storms the week prior to their arrival, some of the transport had been affected by damaged bridges and landslides.

'Ow! Jolly thing.' Ruby lay on the ground holding her ankle.

'What's happened, are you okay?' Kate ran to her side.

'I've twisted my ankle badly on the loose stones.'

Jamie stood over her looking at her leg. 'If only we were near a river, we could apply a cold compress.'

Kate helped her on her feet. 'Let's take a break for a while. Will you be able to walk? If not, we could camp here somewhere until tomorrow. A bus should come through then.' 'No, the swelling's not so bad. I can walk, just not that fast. I don't want to camp out here, I'd rather press on.'

Rick took over as if he was their leader.

'Tell you what ... I'll walk with Ruby slowly until she is feeling a bit better. You two carry on and we'll meet up with you in Atambua. It can't be that far now. What do you think Ruby?'

'I suppose so. I wouldn't mind waiting a bit longer for the swelling to go down.' She would rather it had been Jamie who had made the offer. She even felt tempted to ask if he would stay instead of Rick but didn't want to rock the boat or make a fool of herself.

Ruby sat with Rick on a patch of sandy terrain, giving Ruby's ankle time to let the swelling go down. Jamie had given her a facecloth soaked in water before he went off with Kate.

After half an hour, she stood up, looking around her.

'What's up, mate? What are you looking at?' Rick asked.

'I need to go and water a tree!' Her face went red. She hadn't foreseen this kind. 'I'll go over there behind those bushes and you stay here!'

'Surely you can trust me by now, you silly tart.'

Ruby was not happy about being alone in his company. It had dawned on her that she had placed herself in a precarious position and had been far too trusting.

She trudged with a slight limp across the sandy terrain to a clump of trees. Five minutes later when she walked out from behind a tree, she expected to find Rick waiting for her in the same place she left him.

There was no sign of Rick. The area was silent and empty. Ruby felt butterflies in her stomach as her anxiety grew.

'Come out, you stupid goat! Stopping playing games!' There was no sound, not a flicker of movement. Ruby realised he was playing some kind of a mean trick. Probably vengeance when he became aware of her obvious disdain for his arrogance, compared to her warm response to amiable Jamie. She shuddered. Had he really walked off, or was he about to jump out at her right now?

The pain in her ankle subsided as her anger distracted her from the injury. She was annoyed about the unexpected situation she had found herself. What if he has completely abandoned her and left her alone in the bush?

She plodded her way along the lonely road on the verge of tears, admonishing herself that she thought for a moment that Rick was to be trusted. She should have trusted her initial instincts about this man.

She walked for about ten minutes when she suddenly heard a scuffle in the nearby bushes. 'Well, well, look who we have here!' Rick had jumped out from behind a palm tree. 'Don't worry, I haven't abandoned you. I told the others I would look after you,' he said with a wry smile. Ruby was steaming with exasperation.

She didn't want to spend any more time in his company but also didn't want to walk to Atambua alone. The others were nowhere in sight.

They walked towards the river, and in the distance, Ruby could see people standing on the side of the road. To her delight, there were vehicles parked on the side of the road too, including a minibus. As they drew closer, she could see Jamie and Kate sitting under a tree, chatting with one of the locals.

'Hey, you two, we thought you'd never catch up. We were about to send a search party.' Jamie stood up and walked towards them.

Ruby was so happy to be freed from Rick's unpleasant company. Although he hadn't tried anything really sinister. That would have been disastrous in such a remote area.

'How is your ankle feeling? I'll bet it's aching after such a long walk? We were going to get someone to go back and pick you up.' Kate looped her arm in Ruby's.

'I'm okay ... I'll talk to you later.' Ruby nodded in Rick's direction and rolled her eyes.

'Hey, gang— we have a ride to Atambua. I've managed to get a good deal too.' Jamie stood pointing in the direction of a large truck.

They arrived at Atambua Backpackers and Ario their driver had arrived a few hours before them.

As Ruby glanced around the room in the women's dorm, her arms fell limp then she screwed up her nose. She looked at the walls. They were unpainted and a musty smell like old socks emanated from the walls. She cringed at the sight of the worn, tatty mattresses and wanted to tell the others she would rather look around for alternative accommodation. Even though it was cheap, it was certainly nasty.

'Yuk, there are even cockroaches here.' Kate's upper lip curled in disgust. 'Huge ones at that!'

'I'm out of here tomorrow, but I'm too tired to think about it right now. After we've eaten I'm going to sleep.' Ruby started unpacking her sleeping bag searching for her night attire. She rummaged in her rucksack for her first aid pack, took out a crepe bandage, and wrapped her ankle.

She was up early after sleeping soundly. Her ankle was back to normal. She grabbed a quick bite to eat downstairs then wandered outside. She noticed a wooden seat within a lush garden full of brightly coloured hibiscus flowers. As she sat there meditating, she started to feel uncomfortable about the lack of spiritual direction in her life. How did she end up travelling with these men? It unsettled her.

When she used to help her parents out at Peace Haven retreat in Cromwell Mead, New Zealand, she always felt close to God and that she was living by faith. Now she was not so sure. She remembered the last day before she left to travel overseas with Kate. She had gone for a run and as she passed her local church, she bumped into her vicar who had expressed his disapproval of her randomly doing this big overseas trip.

He had said to her, 'Remember, Ruby it was Peter who was the rock that moved. Jesus didn't move.'

Up until this point in her life, Ruby had found it difficult to fathom what her vicar had meant by this comment and his disapproving glance. Now it made sense. Was she in God's will or just doing her own thing? She asked for more direction and guidance for her life. She was unsure of where she was heading.

'Ruby, is that where you've got to? Hurry and pack up. Ario is leaving in half an hour.

'Good! I can't get out of here quick enough.'

Chapter Five

The journey down the island to Kupang took nearly seven hours. They stopped overnight in a primitive hotel in Kefamenanu and took another minibus to Kupang in the morning.

'I'm glad we booked that flight to Bali before we left Dili. It appears full.' Kate stood looking around the departure lounge for a seat. 'I'm so tired and dying for a decent feed.'

'Me too. I hear the food is so cheap and healthy in Bali. We just have to be careful where we eat. I have a list of places a friend gave me that appear alright.' Ruby took out the list and a banana, quickly eating the fruit before going through customs.

***

Bali was a welcome treat after travelling through primitive Timor. They were relieved to have arrived. The country was more geared up for tourists with many popular resorts scattered around the island.

They stayed at a lodge near Kuta beach where the girls spent most of their time scanning the clothing markets, while the men went off swimming and kayaking.

They were harassed by vendors— women carrying baskets on their heads full of sarongs and tropical beachwear. They just wouldn't leave the girls alone, practically begging them to buy their wares.

'Hey, girls— guess what we've been offered by a few kids further down the beach. These young boys ware selling marijuana. We were horrified! It's a wonder they don't get caught.' Jamie pointed to some cute Balinese boys aged around eight who were walking towards them in the distance.

'That's terrible. I've heard that the underworld gets going at night on this beach.... drugs, prostitution etc. I read that western women come here for sex and many of the young men on the beach looking for sex are married. It's pretty corrupt.'

'Doesn't really enthral me to spend a lot of time in this place then. Not really up my alley.' Kate frowned.

'Hold on ... just wait till you see the amazing beaches further around the coast and Turtle Island. We can go there tomorrow if everyone is keen.' Jamie could see they needed inspiring.

Ruby was fascinated with the spectacular sunsets. She woke early each morning to sit on the beach to pray. She couldn't stop thinking about the young boys selling drugs. What kind of homes would they come from? What bothered her most was that everyone there took it for granted.

At the end of the week, they were all fed up with the commercialism on the island. Denpasar was busy and the traffic seemed to have no rules, creating chaos.

They hired motor-cycles and rode far into the hills to Kintamani away from the roaring crowd. Ruby rode with Kate on the back and Jamie rode with Rick. That was their whole reason for being in South East Asia, to visit remote areas and to see how the third world countries live, experiencing different cultures. But with all the tourism, Bali had become overly westernised.

The road up the mountain was interesting as they passed people working in rice paddies. Rick and Jamie were riding up ahead. Rick turned and waved to the girls, pointing towards a procession that was on its way towards them and they slowed down.

'Hey, look— it must be some kind of a funeral procession. Look at those amazing coloured costumes.' Kate stopped to take it all in. 'Wow! How on earth do they balance all that fruit on their head? Amazing!'

They took photographs discreetly from a distance so as not to offend the grieving parties.

Kintamani offered an even greater attraction. Mount Batur volcano had recently had a small eruption. There were guided tours to the crater, but the group decided it was too expensive. They admired the view, taking loads of photographs, then after enjoying a late lunch in one of the local restaurants, they spent the rest of the day sight-seeing around the village.

'We'd better start making tracks,' Jamie said, concerned about driving a motorbike in the dark on unfamiliar roads.

Ruby was eager to get to Bangkok where the group of four would disperse.

***

They flew from Bali to Yogyakarta and endured yet another arduous, hot and claustrophobic train journey— destination Jakarta. Both the girls were quickly losing interest in this big overland travel. It certainly was not for the faint-hearted, and even Kate was beginning to think she wasn't as tough as she thought she was.

'Now girls— don't say I don't do you any favours,' said Rick. Ruby cringed at his so-called brain waves and ideas.

'I've managed to get us on board a cargo boat from Jakarta to Padang. We'll have to sleep in our hammocks on the deck as there's no cabin accommodation on this cheap trip.'

'I've heard they are pretty grubby, but I suppose it's not for long and other transport is so costly,' said Jamie, waiting for everyone's reaction. The girls' faces dropped.

The trip to Padang was rough on the ship, with a storm brewing soon after they arrived on the deck.

'Hurry girls.' Jamie spoke with a sense of urgency. 'We need to get the hammocks strung up on that steel girder.' The men helped the girls get sorted first then took care of their own hammocks. They sat down and ate some of the provisions they bought in Jakarta.

'Oh no, it's my turn now Ruby. Where's the ladies' room? I've been drinking heaps of water all day.'

'I saw the crew use one over there near the lifeboats.' Kate walked towards the door where she was directed. She stopped aghast and turned around. Walking towards Ruby she quickly looked for an alternative.

'It was so disgusting, the smell made me retch,' she said holding her hand over her nose.

'There's always the ocean as long as you don't fall in.' Kate slinked away somewhere out of sight.

During the overnight trip to Padang, a few female university students had also embarked on this trip. To Ruby's disgust, one of the girls agreed to sleep with the Indonesian Captain to get a free ticket for the journey. He was married, Ruby later learned. She also couldn't understand why any intelligent girl would want to treat herself like that.

As the sun started to go down, a gentle breeze started blowing. It was welcome at first after the penetrating heat, but the wind started to get stronger. During the middle of the night, Ruby woke with a huge thud and pain in her back. 'Oh no, my stupid hammock has spliced. I think I've broken my front tooth. It's made a hole in my lip too.' Jamie heard her yell out and ran to her aid. 'You look a bit shocked.' He waved a torch in her direction. 'Have you hurt yourself apart from the tooth?'

'My tailbone hurts, feels a bit numb. I think it's only bruised though.' She couldn't understand why she had been so accident prone during this trip.

'It's too dark to do anything now.' Jamie shone the torch around the deck. 'I could wander up onto the Bridge and I'm sure to find someone who can give us some ice.'

'No, please ... I don't want any fuss. But thank you, it's very kind of you, Jamie. I'll have to sleep on the ground now and when we get to Bangkok, I'll get my tooth sorted and get my back checked out.'

Jamie took out his rubber sleeping mat from his rucksack and lay it on the ground for Ruby. She climbed into her sleeping bag and drifted off to sleep as she was soothed by the waves lapping against the boat.

They disembarked in Padang, surrounded by Indonesian men leering at the two girls who were dressed only in denim shorts and sleeveless blouses. They had not checked out the cultural mores of that area and overlooked that the men are mostly Muslim and not used to women showing bare skin.

'They are ghastly the way they are following us and leering,' Kate grumbled. 'I'm glad we have Rick and Jamie with us still. We would definitely not have been able to travel overland in areas like this on our own.'

Ruby couldn't wait for the rough and exhausting travel to come to an end. It had been such a culture shock for her.

Chapter Six

The trip from Padang to Medan took the whole day. At the backpacker lodge that night Ruby woke around midnight with sharp stomach pains. For the next three days, she lay low with dysentery, only able to drink boiled water and consume steamed rice.

Day three of their stay in Medan prior to the flight to Bangkok, Ruby still lay stretched out on her bed feeling completely debilitated from lack of food. Kate popped her head in the door to ask if she would go with her to the local market. She'd heard from the tourists that denim jeans were cheap there, and they could buy beautiful batik sarongs at a low cost. They'd make great gifts for her family, but she just couldn't muster enough strength to go out.

'You go Kate. I bought a couple of sarongs in Bali, and I can probably go to the markets in Bangkok. I'm feeling a bit weak and woozy.'

'Are you sure you are going to be okay by yourself?'

'I'd rather try and sleep as I didn't get any last night.'

Kate took off to the market with Jamie and Rick, carrying her small daypack and camera.

Ruby was woken by a man's voice at her door. 'Hey, excuse me, sorry to disturb you. My name's Mike. Have you seen Rick around? He's an old mate of mine. We used to share the same flat in London years ago. I wanted to give him a small package before I fly out to India this afternoon.'

'Sorry, he's left an hour ago for the markets and a bit of sight-seeing.'

'I need to leave this with him, he's expecting it. Can you give it to him please?'

Ruby was still lying flat on her bed. 'Poke it into the empty pocket at the side of my rucksack there.' She pointed at her rucksack leaning against the door of her room.

'Ah, great, thanks. Let him know Mike left it for him. He'll know what I mean.'

***

The next day they all packed up ready to fly out to Penang. When they arrived at the airport, to their surprise, there were military police scattered around the walls holding machine guns.

After they boarded the plane, Ruby suddenly remembered the package she forgot to give to Rick and whispered her dilemma to Kate. 'You had better tell him as soon as the plane lands. Do you know what was in the package?'

'No, Mike didn't say. Probably a gift he bought for his family or something like that, I guess.' Ruby thought that maybe she had been too trusting.

As soon as the plane arrived, she disembarked and ran over to tell Rick.

'What! Why didn't you tell me before we got on the plane? You haven't still got the package, have you?' He bellowed. His eyes became like big black pools.

'It's still in my pack. I forgot to take it out. I was feeling unwell and lying on my bed when he dropped it off.'

'Oh no, we're in trouble now.' He leaned against the wall, his hands behind his head, looking into the air as if he was searching for answers.

He started to tell them that the small package contained a kilo of cannabis which he and Mike had been smoking in Medan. As Mike was flying out first, he left it for Rick to use until he flew out the next day. He was to dispose of it discreetly before he got on the plane.

'You stupid fool Rick! Look what trouble this has caused. We didn't even know you smoked dope. Jamie, did you know about this?' Ruby was red in the face, feeling angry and powerless. 'No, Ruby, I promise ... you idiot Rick! This is serious, mate, very serious.'

'I know, I know! I'll sort it.'

Ruby had already grabbed her rucksack from the baggage pickup area and now had to go through customs.

As they sat down trying to work out what to do, Kate noticed that a female customs inspector was working at one end of the conveyor belt and appeared to just be checking hand luggage. She saw Ruby and beckoned her to bring her bags over. Ruby cowered, feeling like she wanted to vomit.

'Just your hand luggage please madam, let me see that.' The woman searched Ruby's hand luggage meticulously. 'You can go.' The woman smiled and greeted the next one in the queue without asking to check Ruby's backpack.

She was free to go. She couldn't believe it. God had his hand on her because she was innocent. He had been looking after her. She quietly said a quick prayer, with a heart full of thanks.

Ruby stayed angry with Rick until he departed and never wanted to see him again. He seemed to get the hint, not only from Ruby but from the rest of the group too. Jamie must have given him a right rollicking, Ruby thought as Rick muttered a weak 'sorry' and shot off out of the airport to everyone's relief.

Ruby had a sudden thought about how she could get rid of the contraband from her pack. She noticed a large wooden planter with a robust, bushy tree in the corner of the airport near the exit. It was far enough from the armed police for them not to notice. She sat on the side of the trough, put her hand in the side pocket of her pack, and slipped the packet into the trough.

'Let's go, walk fast, and don't stop,' Ruby said to the others. They took off fast as lightning, not looking back until they were a good distance from the airport. They had gone unnoticed.

'I knew there was something dodgy about him. He wasn't a nice person and I'm glad he has gone,' said Ruby, very shaken by the daunting experience.

'I'm so sorry, Ruby I had no idea he was smoking dope, honest I didn't. He's not the person I knew in London when we were flatting. He seems to have changed. I really am sorry. We used to run a course together at the Holy Trinity Church in London and became good friends. When he asked me to travel with him, it had been some time since I'd seen him.'

Ruby could see he was feeling awkward about the whole situation. 'Why don't we all go down to Malacca and stay at the beach for a week? It'll be a break from travelling. We can spend a few days in Penang, as there's a lot to do here. We can take a train to Kuala Lumpur and another train to Malacca.'

'How long are these train rides? I'm getting a bit weary now.'

'Penang to Kuala Lumpur takes about five hours and about an hour and a half from there lies beautiful Malacca. You'll love it, honest you will.'

***

Kuala Lumpur station was busy. There was a half hour wait before the train set off for Malacca. Numerous women walked past the train windows carrying heavy colourful baskets piled high on their heads, hoping for a quick sale before the train pulled out.

As Ruby watch the sights through the windows, she was taken aback. Her eyes widened. She stopped abruptly, leaning against the window and sat bolt upright craning her neck to see out.

The target of her glance confirmed what she thought she had seen. There were small children begging. Some of them were missing an arm or a leg and the odd one appeared to have an eye plucked out. She saw a boy of about ten, carrying a baby on his back in a sling. Most of the children appeared dirty, skinny, and unkempt.

Ruby swallowed a lump that formed in her throat. There was a heaviness in the pit of her stomach. She wanted to take them home to a safe place and take care of them. But there were too many. A bottomless pit of poverty. She was fed up with the injustice of it all and couldn't get it off her mind.

'That's what I was telling you about.' Kate elbowed her. 'Some parents deliberately maim their children so they can beg and bring in an income.'

Ruby slumped back into the corner of her seat closing her eyes, hoping the horror of the reality of it all would just disappear. Her sheltered upbringing did not prepare her for such stark horrors.

Chapter Seven

The journey to Malacca was more comfortable than travelling in Indonesia. The trains in Malaysia were clean and less primitive and there were fewer passengers going to Malacca that day.

'Wow, take a look at that.' Kate jumped out of her seat and pointed to the long stretch of white sand and coconut palms. The sea was a spectacle of sparkling azure blue water—similar to some of the beaches back home. In this remote part of Malaysia, the coastline is a real find for the intrepid traveller. The girls couldn't believe their eyes.

They arrived at the station platform looking for a station guard to tell them the directions to their private beach accommodation. He pointed to a man standing next to a car at the station entrance. The driver approached them smiling. 'Gidday folks, I'm Hugh, the local cab driver.'

He spoke with a strong English accent.

'Where are you from?' Jamie shook his hand. 'Are you English?'

'Yep, I hail from Cornwall, but I've been living here for the last five years. It's too idyllic to leave for cold England.'

'Are you able to take us to our beach hut a little way down the coast?' Kate asked.

'Sure, no problem, jump in. I'll throw your backpacks in the boot.'

A short distance around the coast, they saw their beach hut. It had a thatched roof and was set back amongst the palms on a stretch of pure white sand and turquoise water.

'What a sight for sore eyes!' Jamie had his camera out, taking photos through the car window.

They tipped Hugh generously and told him they would need a taxi ride back to the station at the end of the week.

'I'm off for a swim after I've unpacked.' Ruby tried to run down the sandy path to their hut, forgetting she was carrying a pack that was almost the same size as her. She wished she'd taken her father's advice and bought a smaller one, as she only needed summer clothing and most people buy it from the markets.

They sat around enjoying the shade of a towering coconut palm, eating produce they had bought at the market in Kuala Lumpur.

'Last one in the water can clean the fish I catch later.' Jamie ran for the waves and dived in.

'I'll wait a bit to see if the sharks eat you first then decide,' said Kate, eyes fixated on the water as though she was searching for the sign of a shark fin.

They spent the afternoon snorkelling, studying the marine life they had never experienced before. Afterwards, they frolicked in the warm water, ducking and diving like children, pushing each other under.

Ruby threw her towel down on the sand and sat on it. Jamie came and sat down beside her, drying himself off. 'This really is a piece of paradise, so remote and untouched it seems.' He stood up, staring at their panoramic surroundings.

'Yes, you're right— a perfect piece of God's creation.' Ruby was relaxed about being open about her faith, now that she no longer risked being taunted by Rick.

James started picking up shells off the beach while Ruby stayed in deep thought. She began thinking about these little pieces of paradise on earth. *They are quixotic, or utopian. One day lots of tourists will discover this and they'll come here in their hoards on buses. Huge ugly hotels or apartments will be built and one will have to be a millionaire to stay here.* She pondered more on this theme as she sat on her towel, letting the sun dry her skin after the swim. *There has to be more to life than trying to find utopia on a planet that is decaying and becoming polluted, destroyed by man. Even the wild animals are being poached and horrifically mutilated, while their parts are sold as trophies or aphrodisiacs in some countries. God's perfect creation annihilated by greed and capitalism everywhere. What's it all about, God?*

'Hey! Don't go to sleep over there, Ruby, you'll get burnt to a frazzle.' Kate walked up and grabbed her hand, pulling her to her feet to hurry her up. 'Let's get our beds ready and find the ladies. I heard from my friend that the huts have a long drop at the back of them, with proper seats on top. Absolute luxury I'd say. We don't have much light except for our gas lanterns, so perhaps we can put one of them out there so we're not fumbling around in the dark.'

Kate had already unpacked her lantern and walked along to Jamie's room to ask if they could use one of his lamps.

Early the next morning, Jamie walked along the beach to the hut carrying a sack with fish.

'Goodness! That's enough to feed us for the next few days.' Kate had just woken. 'Not bad for your first catch of the day.' She seemed impressed by Jamie's attempt to catch her attention.

For the rest of their time at the hut, they just swam, ate, and fished. They lived simply on dried beans, rice, fish, dried vegetables, and tropical fruit. By the time they were ready to leave their idyllic spot, they were rested and recovered from their exhausting overland travels and were ready to move forward.

***

A week later, the taxi arrived to take them back to the railway station.

'Howdy folks, how did it all go? Hugh poked his head around the corner of the hut. 'Can I help carry anything up to the car?' His face dropped as though he had regretted asking when he saw the size of their packs.

'No thanks, Hugh— we have all become an old hand at carrying our packs now.' Ruby said, although struggling to get her pack on her back.

The sea and hot sun had worn them out, but Ruby felt exhilarated after all the swimming and walking. The train's gentle motion rocked her to sleep during the ride back to Kuala Lumpur.

There was a large taxi rank next to the station and they took a cab straight to the airport in time for their flight to Bangkok.

At last the endless travelling was almost over. It had been far too long for Ruby, three months on the road. She had started losing her sense of purpose. Surely there must be more to life than self-gratification through extended holidays and adventures. Seeking fun and pleasure seems purpose-less, she thought. She yearned to be of some value to her fellow man and couldn't wait to make use of herself at Rescue Net in Thailand.

***

Jamie stayed on in Bangkok at the backpackers for a few days sight-seeing with the girls, then left to go home to Auckland. Ruby gave him a few gifts to take back to her family. He said he was keen to drive down to Peace Haven in Cromwell Mead to visit them. The girls spent the rest of the morning in the botanic gardens. Afterwards, Kate collected her mail from the local Post Restante.

'Kate— why don't you stay on with me at Rainbow Haven, my parent's Safe House in Bangkok? I'll show you what we do, and if you're keen you could help with some of the education programs.'

'Why kind of programs? What do I know about human trafficking or prostitution? I'll see when I get there.'

They'd picked up a few steamed barbeque pork buns, Ruby's favourites, and iced Kachang with red beans and rose syrup.

There was a wooden bench in the botanic gardens where they could sit and eat their lunch. Ruby continued to try to talk Kate into doing some casual work at the refuge.

'The children at Rainbow Haven come to us from all over. From India, Nepal, Cambodia, Vietnam and the whole of Thailand. They are all under seventeen. The team at Rescue Net work with the local police and go in undercover then arrest the brothel owners and close the places down.'

Ruby started to realise the profound courage her parents had displayed at setting this organisation up. She could make a worthwhile contribution towards the cause if she stayed to get involved with them for a while. 'Please, Kate, come and help us out for a while. You'll be given food and accommodation at Rainbow Haven if you provide training and service.'

'What have I got to offer them?'

'We have a medical clinic next door for the residents. Many of them come to us having been badly abused and some of them have been tortured or mutilated for trying to escape. There are young boys too. Many girls end up pregnant. We provide maternity care with subsidies from the government.'

'But what would I be able to do?'

'Those who are in recovery with injuries from assaults, sexual diseases, respiratory problems and deformities, all need the input of a qualified nurse. We've not been able to get nurses interested in our establishment.'

'Oh, so that's what you are getting at. Why can't you find a local nurse?'

'People are afraid that if they work for the Net, they'll get reprisals from associates of the brothel owners and become targeted—but it's not true. The community is supportive and protective of the work we are doing, and none of the staff has ever been targeted.'

'What an amazing organisation. I suppose I could give it a go. I've been working in the tropical disease ward at my hospital and could be of some help for a while.'

'You said you wanted to go back to Bonalbo to get to know Merv a bit more. Have you heard from him?'

'Yes— he wrote and asked me if I'd like to help out in his clinic. I suppose I could do that after I leave Thailand. I have to say I was quite impressed with him.' Her cheeks flushed.

'So, I noticed … good on you girl, you go for it. Just feel free to stay at Rainbow Haven and go when you want.'

***

The bus ride to Rainbow Haven on the outskirts of the city took an hour and the girls almost slept a whole day after they arrived. The constant travel in the heat on vehicles without air conditioning was overwhelming. Ruby almost cried with relief when their long trip was over. Both the girls were exhausted and practically fell through the doors of Rainbow Haven. After they were allocated the room that they shared, they both took a long nap.

At Ruby starting waking up and moving around, there was a gentle knock at the door.

'Good morning, Ruby. Here are some bananas and green tea for you both. My name's Gamon. I'm the female coordinator.'

Kate sat up shielding eyes as the sun poured through the doorway.

'Hello, thanks for the food. I'm Ruby and this is Kate.'

'It's just a snack for you. We'll have a communal meal at five in that building over there.' She pointed through the window.

The rest of the week, the girls took the time to recover from their arduous trip. They had been introduced to all the staff and residents. It took them almost the whole week to get back on their feet.

Gamon took time to orientate the girls to the program. She loved talking to them and began to open up about her own life.

'I've been on the staff for about two years, though Rainbow Haven has been my home since I was fifteen. I've been researching HIV in sex workers and just completed my thesis.' As she spoke, she puffed her chest out and held her long neck high like a swan.

'That sounds like an amazing achievement, the team must be so pleased to have your help. I'm sure you and Kate will have a lot in common.'

'You'll have to tell me all about your research Gamon. By the way—what does your name mean in Thai?' Kate asked with an affable smile.

'It means "from the heart".'

'That's lovely. Would you mind telling us how you ended up at Rescue Net?' Ruby glanced at her gingerly.

'My parents were killed in riots and I lived on the streets for a while.'

'Didn't you have any relatives who could take you in?' Ruby wanted to give her a hug but restrained herself.

'My Aunt and Uncle who lived in the hill country found me and took me in for a few months.'

She sat on the end of Kate's bed and hung her head as she continued to tell her story.

'I thought I was going to be living with them, but one day a car arrived at their house with a mean looking man and his wife. My Aunt said I was going with them to a lovely hotel in the city to work as a waitress to earn lots of money. They said they were too poor to look after me.'

'How did you end up in the brothel? Kate appeared perplexed.

'At first, they started getting me to clear tables in the hotel restaurant until one day the boss said I'd earned a promotion and they needed me to work at escorting wealthy businessmen to dinner and to serve their drinks. The owners gradually lured me into prostitution and threatened I would get hurt if I tried to leave.'

'Look, you don't have to talk about it if it is making you uncomfortable.' Ruby glanced hard at Kate as if to tell her to let it rest. Kate nodded, giving her a half smile and went quiet.

Gamon continued, 'they didn't pay me wages and said I had to earn my food and accommodation. My relatives had abandoned me so I was trapped there.'

Ruby studied Gamon as she spoke. The young woman had an amazing maturity for her years but Ruby wondered what kind of horrific scars lay hidden deep inside her heart. How could such a young girl survive that? The girls just sat and waited for her to finish.

'It turned out the hotel was just a cover for an elaborate prostitution racket. Rescue Net went in undercover and found me. The hotel owners were arrested.'

Ruby tried to change the subject.

'Why did the staff at the safe house call you "from the heart"?'

'I started running around helping others who seemed worse off than myself. I had a sophisticated wardrobe of clothes given to me by the hotel owners. When I went to university, I distributed the clothes to the poorer girls. I also started teaching the children who had been denied education. I just felt compassion for them.'

Ruby found it perplexing to think that this young woman, who was in her early twenties, could reach out to others when she had suffered so much rejection, abandonment, and abuse from others, including her own family. Gamon also confided in Ruby that when she had fallen pregnant at fourteen years old, the brothel owner had deliberately kicked her in the abdomen and she lost the baby.

'I was so overwhelmed with the unconditional love of our benefactors— your parents Cherie and Lyon that I wanted to come to know their God and became converted. That's when I was filled with this overwhelming desire to help others who'd been in my situation.'

Ruby and Kate knew that Rescue Net had caught a "big fish" with Gamon who sounded like an amazingly strong woman.

'You have an unshakeable faith.' Ruby gently stroked Gamon's forearm then pulled away, realising her display of affection may have been a bit premature for such an abuse victim.

'Come on Kate— I'll introduce you to all the staff and go over our policies etc. You'll have to sign a kind of employment contract with myself and Gamon before you can start. Gamon is in charge of the centre now with several other Thai staff, and my parents oversee the program.'

Chapter Eight

Julian Page had been working at Rainbow Haven for the last six years. He'd been employed as a child welfare worker in London where he'd also studied criminology. He started out doing aid work in Cambodia when he saw Rescue Net advertising for someone to manage the centre in Bangkok. He now heads up the team of men and women who accompany the police to conduct the raids on the brothels.

***

Kate had been working with Ruby at Rainbow Haven for just over a month when strange things started to happen, sinister things.

One morning Julian had noticed Ruby walking back from the Saturday market, he ran up to her, taking hold of her jute shopping bags. Her face was pale and she shook.

'Oh, it's okay, I can manage. I've just carried them two blocks.'

In a gentlemanly fashion, he took them regardless. Her mouth stretched wide in a full smile. Her eyes even smiled.

'Julian, some weird man has been following me at the market and deliberately tripped me up. All my groceries went sprawling over the street. I've never seen him before, but he looked pretty angry and muttered something in a strange dialect.' Her voice quavered a little. Her hand started to shake as she swiped her fringe from her eyes.

'Let me know if it happens again. You'd better take someone else with you down to the market until we know if this is a coincidence or it was planned.'

Julian acted protectively towards Ruby, as he knew the hidden dangers of the work that they did. Up until now, they

47

had not had any trouble. But they had recently raided a particular brothel in Bangkok, a huge tourist attraction and a real favourite amongst the perverts who prey after youngsters.

'It's possible that there's a syndicate operating in the area,' Julian explained to Ruby and Kate. 'The closing of this brothel will have angered the owner's associates, who are still roaming free. Many of them go very much unnoticed. They have their money invested in multiple brothels and casinos throughout Thailand.'

'What are they likely to do now?' For the first time, Ruby was beginning to feel the threat of such a risky operation.

'They may get vindictive and try to use scare tactics in the hope that we'll shut down our operation and move us away. That's why we should take extra precautions when roaming around the city. Rescue Net is not just an ordinary charity or aid organisation. It's a serious law enforcing body that plays a dominant role with the local police and Thailand's Central Intelligence Agency.'

'Why haven't they been shut down in the past if child prostitution has been going on?'

Kate's cheeks looked bloodless. She started to scratch her head obsessively. 'I'm finding it hard to believe that the authorities could turn such a blind eye to such things.'

'There have even been some Generals who have supported brothels as well as corrupt policemen, but the country is now getting on top of such rackets.'

'Well— I admire your parents Ruby, for setting up such a risky organisation. It took real guts.' Kate began to think that there was a lot more to Ruby now than met the eye.

The girls decided to stay in their room for the afternoon, catching up on mail, and packaging up some items they bought in Indonesia to send home to their families.

That night the humidity was high. Ruby sat up and threw off her light blanket. She was grateful for the insect screen covering her wide open window. She and Kate both had their own upstairs room now.

During the night, Rescue Net's security guards did their rounds vigilantly as usual. One guard monitored the inside of the building where the rescued children were in residence, while the second guard monitored the outside. They were both armed.

The large compound where the residence stood, had been beautifully landscaped with an abundance of stately trees and tropical flowers of every colour imaginable. Surrounding the park-like gardens stood a high fence covered with barbed wire to keep out villains who try to poach the girls and take them back to the brothels.

Though the residents were not prisoners, they were closely guarded during the first year of their recovery. Later they were re-housed to another part of the country close to the university or to their new places of employment. For some, it took longer than a year to get back on their feet.

'Ruby, guess what? I received an affectionate letter from you know who! Merv wants to know how long I'll be staying on here.'

'Oh, that's what I thought would happen as he didn't look as though he was going to let you get away.' Ruby was elated with her friend's news.

'Well, I don't know what to do ... I mean he's asking if I'd seriously consider going back to work with him in his clinic.'

'But you're used to working with humans, not animals.' Ruby was surreptitiously hoping her friend wouldn't abandon her post just yet. She also felt she could do with some support.

'I've always loved animals and I'd rather have become a veterinary nurse, but my parents insisted I stick to medical nursing.'

'What are you going to tell him then?'

'I'm considering transferring my nursing Degree to a Diploma in Remote Veterinary Nursing. Merv said he'll help me to apply.'

'Oh, that's interesting … when will all this take place?'

'Well, if it's okay with you, I could stay on here until the academic year begins in March. That'll give you time to find another nurse to take my place.'

'Mmm … and where will you stay when you get there?'

'Jane's Mum would like to rent her spare room out. Jane's working on a contract for several months as a remote nurse in the outback. Merv said she has offered her room to me if I'm keen.'

'Sounds okay to me. Hey— I'm tuckered out. Perhaps we can talk about it again tomorrow. I'm off to bed.' Ruby knew she didn't exactly sound over the moon about Jane's promising friendship with Merv. It's just that she had hoped her friend would stay on at Rainbow Haven a lot longer. Still, perhaps she can make new friends, here in Rainbow Haven.

***

Towards midnight, a deafening noise like firecrackers thundered against Ruby's eardrums. The whole building shook. Frightened girls started running around turning on lights, screaming.

'What on earth was that? It sounded like a bomb!' Ruby ran to the window.

'Get away from the windows!' Julian called out as he ran along the corridor. 'It's okay— don't panic. Some nutter threw a firebomb into the laundry. No one is hurt, but the children are racing around everywhere. One of the guards caught him as he was running off. Help me get the little ones settled and talk to them. Tell them he's been caught.'

Ruby and Kate made the children some tea and handed around cookies they had baked earlier as a treat.

'This is the last thing they all need right now. What will happen to him now ... who is he?' Ruby looked at Julian who appeared calm and cool-headed.

'He's one of the thugs who belong to that syndicate who ran the Bangkok brothel— the one that used that flash Hotel, Tropicana as a cover. It was a huge hit to the industry when we closed that one down. It provided a lot of jobs for locals and they ran illegal rackets.'

'Will there be more reprisals, do you think?' Ruby was beginning to think this was a huge drawback for Rescue Net.

'No, I don't think there will be. The police here have very powerful methods of persuasion when extracting the truth from these criminals. They'll rout out the main culprits and deal with them in such a way that they won't dare try this caper again.'

'I suppose these young ones are used to far worse trauma than this.'

'Oh, for sure. This will really be water on a duck's back for a lot of them, compared to other intrusions in their daily lives. They'll bounce back okay, don't you worry.'

Chapter Nine

March arrived quickly. Kate was ready to fly back to Sydney and take the train to meet Merv in Bonalbo. Julian helped her load her luggage into his car while Ruby said her goodbyes to Kate.

'I hope I'm not letting you down, Ruby. You've been so good offering me work here and travelling with me all the way overland. I'm not exactly the easiest travel companion. Thanks so much.'

'That's okay, Kate, I couldn't have done the trip on my own, especially with that awful Rick in tow.'

Kate quietly pulled Ruby aside while Julian was busy packing the car.

'At least you have lovely Julian here to help you. I thought maybe he might have a few designs on you but I didn't want to say. Is it true, do you think?'

Ruby looked at her feet and stammered a little.

'I ... haven't really noticed that. Though I think he's a really sweet guy, quite different from blokes I've met in the past. I need to get to know him better, I suppose.'

'Please promise you'll come and visit me in Bonalbo if I stay on. I'll keep in touch.'

Ruby's heart sank as she waved off her friend. She wondered when she'd see her again.

She felt somewhat lost without Kate. They'd been constant companions for almost a year now and she felt it would not be easy making real friends in Bangkok.

***

Julian arrived back from the airport and caught Ruby's attention as he drove into the carpark. He poked his head through the car window. 'Ruby, do you mind popping into the office for a few minutes? I need to discuss something with you.' He got out of the car and appeared to be holding some official papers in his hand.

Ruby had that sinking feeling in the stomach that she used to get in her school days when she was reprimanded by her teacher.

'Here, grab some coffee, I've just made it.'

'Thanks, I will. What's up is there a problem?'

'Not really, just an update. You know that bloke they caught who threw the firebomb? He confessed— though I'd hate to think how they got the information from him or how they threatened him. Anyway, they have tracked down the whole syndicate from that hotel and they are all in a high-security prison until sentencing.'

'That's fantastic news. We need to let the residents know that.'

'Gamon is at a meeting with them all now.'

There was a huge clamour coming from the downstairs hall and the sound of loud shouts of joy and laughter.

'I knew that would happen. Most of them have been on tenterhooks since the explosion, wondering what would be coming next.'

'Poor things. I feel for them, I really do. We need to try to think of something really uplifting we can do for them right now.'

'That's what I want to talk to you about. I have official documents here from the government who have identified a lot of these victims with help from the Central Investigation Bureau. They have located some of their families in the villages where they were kidnapped from, and will be sending them home.'

'That's marvellous, it's a miracle! They must be so happy, beyond description.'

'This is where you come into it, Ruby. We need a woman to chaperone the children back to their homes. Some will be going to Nepal and others to Myanmar and Cambodia. But many of them have been sold by their relatives who should have been their protectors. The Thai girls mostly come from the rural hill tribes who are very poor and uneducated. They had been sent to the cities to work as waitresses. Unfortunately, they were lured there under false pretences by pimps for prostitution. In those cases, we have to find safe foster families or people who will adopt them.'

Ruby slumped in her chair with her head in her hands at the enormity of the problem. She looked up at him. 'What happens to the poor children after they have been rescued?

'Some of them as young as five had already become sex slaves. A few of them have lost their minds. They'll be adopted out into caring families, as it's not safe for them to return to their relatives. I read that there are over twenty million adults and children who have been trafficked globally.'

With that, Ruby felt sick and quickly lost her appetite—although the aroma of some delicious dish had been wafting through to the office as they spoke.

'Are you happy about chaperoning the children back home to their foster families? Gamon will accompany you to translate and I'll also be with you.'

When Julian said he would be accompanying her, she was elated and her face showed it.

'Of course, no trouble at all. It'll be a privilege to support them.'

'It's all a daunting time for them still. They need a kind woman who they can trust on-board. Thanks, Ruby.'

***

A few months after the residents had gone to their new homes, Rainbow Haven seemed empty when Ruby took a look around. She wondered how long it would be before it would be filled up again.

She went into the laundry and started ironing her blouse, when Julian appeared at the door, enjoying watching her domesticity. 'Time for a break. All work and no play makes Jack a dull boy! Isn't that how the saying goes?'

Ruby stopped ironing and beamed a heart-warming smile at him. 'I know what you mean about all work and no play. I feel like getting out of here for a while. It's my day off.'

'How about accompanying me to a great café in our beautiful botanical gardens. My shout—what do you think?' He moved closer, placing his hand on her arm as if to encourage her to put away the iron.

'That sounds very nice, thank you. I'm almost finished here. I'll meet you out the front in ten minutes.'

The gardens were all in full bloom, a myriad of technicolour—a radiance that Ruby had never seen in a government park reserve before. This was special, and so was the company.

'Ruby, come and look at this, quick.' Julian tugged on her arm, leading her to a tree where brightly coloured birds with lime green and orange plumage were feeding on some insects.

'Look at that—Bee-eaters. Aren't they wonderful mothers?' He surprised her with his random observation. He was referring to a mother bird feeding her baby very close to where they were standing. The fat youngster stood with its mouth wide open while the mother ran over to where the food was then hopped back to its baby several times. The mother bird hardly ate anything.

'Wow, that's amazing!' Ruby was lost for words as they watched. She quietly grabbed her camera.

'How can people say there's no God when you look at this? How can they steadfastly believe that all this began with a bang and not believe in creation and a loving God!'

'Come on girl—let's grab a coffee while there's still some fresh food available. It's so popular here, the cabinet food disappears quickly.' Julian draped an arm across her shoulders as they wandered around a large pond towards the café.

'Good, I'm ravenous right now.' Ruby was surprised by Julian's familiarity but enjoyed the unexpected physical contact.

They sat on the veranda with their food watching the large Asian Openbill bird with pink feet, trying its luck near the fish pond.

'It's good we have Gamon to help us at Rainbow Haven. She's so bright and has such a way with the young girls. We'd be lost without her now, but it's important to keep training others in case she moves on.' Ruby was impressed that Gamon had been giving her private Thai lessons and teaching her about the culture of the hill tribes so she could have a better understanding of the residents they housed.

'I don't know how long she's going to stay with us, but we need to be training someone to take her place. What if she has to suddenly leave us for some reason?'

'I hadn't given that any thought until now. Such workers are easily taken for granted. Hey—would you like an ice-cream? They make great sundaes here.'

They sat under a pink magnolia tree with their ice-cream. Julian leaned over and wiped a drip off her chin with his handkerchief.

Ruby continued. 'Gamon told me she has already been training one of our residents called Isra who is very keen to come on board.'

'You mean that girl who was rescued in a raid when she was four years old?' Julian asked.

'Yes, that's the one.'

'How did she come to be with Rescue Net?'

'Her story is sad. Her parents had abandoned her when they couldn't afford to feed their children anymore. She was then kidnapped off the streets and trafficked to Bangkok, poor thing. When she was picked up off the streets by the brothel owners, they planned to use her for child pornography, as she is very pretty. But she just screamed constantly and couldn't be pacified. They got fed up and threw her in the attic with some older girls. They took care of her, shielded her until the raid took place. She just cried and cried at first, Mum said.'

Ruby stopped for a minute, her eyes transfixed on a large black and white hornbill making a loud noise like a dog barking in the branch above them.

'My parents were involved in the raid. They transported trafficked victims onto a helicopter and flew them out of there. They were assisted by some men from the United Nations. My parents tried to track down her family but couldn't identify her, so my mother called her Isra which means freedom. Now she has grown into a beautiful young woman with a gentle heart. She's completing a criminology degree at a university where Gamon studied.'

There was a sudden chill in the warm tropical breeze that was cooled by the pond. Ruby crossed her arms and shivered. 'I think we should start heading back now.'

Ruby enjoyed the long walk back to Rainbow Haven with Julian. It had been relaxing spending the day with him. It felt like a real date, and he was definitely a man of integrity who shared the same values. She noticed the way he walked, confidently with head up high and straight shoulders. She loved the way he was always so well-groomed, as though he always had a woman preparing his clothes for him. They looked perfectly ironed and his colour coordination appeared impeccable. 'Mmm, very impressive', Ruby said quietly to herself, watching him throw a crust of bread from one of his sandwiches to the large white goose following them.

'I like your smart blue shirt. Is it silk?' Ruby controlled the urge to rub her hands over the garment.

'Yes, I picked it up at a market, actually. It was quite cheap, to be honest. All clothes are inexpensive over here.'

'Well, it goes well with your beige cargo pants.'

Ruby admired his taste in clothes. Not that it was high on the agenda for her, as men go. She looked mainly at the heart but did like to know a man was clean and tidy and took care of his personal appearance. To her, it showed not only self-respect but also regard for the company he shared.

'I have to confess, clothes are one of my weaknesses. Though I suppose it could be drugs or wild women, so that's pretty mild, eh?' He winked at her and again draped an arm over her shoulders, this time more affectionately.

'Ruby, I received a letter from your parents about our move to the countryside. They want me to check out a hotel that has become a mortgagee sale. Why don't you come with me? I told your folks that you are so much part of our community here, that it might be hard for them to get you back to Cromwell Mead. They thought you were just going to help out briefly.'

'Sure, I'll come with you. Mum wrote to me about the property too and said she would get you to check it out, as they want to make an offer before it gets snapped up. The price has dropped to rock bottom I believe. Mum said the owners were desperate to sell it and that you were handling it.'

'Great, I hope we can get it as it sounds perfect for Rainbow Haven. By the way— why did your parents name the safe house Rainbow Haven?'

'Oh, that means a sanctuary of hope. Do you remember that story in the Bible about Noah's flood? After the flood, God said he would never flood the earth again and destroy all life, and as a sign of his promise, he said to look for the rainbow. The rainbow is a sign of hope and a future.'

'Perhaps we can also call the children who come to us, the rainbow children, what do you think?'

'Hey, great idea! Why don't you bring it up at our next meeting, particularly with Gamon and Isra as they have been involved with Rescue Net the longest?'

Ruby and Julian arrived at Rainbow Haven in time for dinner. They had walked a long way from the botanical gardens and Ruby was glad of the exercise.

It seemed peaceful at Rainbow Haven without all the children but Ruby missed them, especially seeing the different ones blossom and flourish after all the tender loving care they had received from Rescue Net.

As she settled down for the night, it was difficult for her to get off to sleep. She just couldn't stop thinking about the pleasant afternoon she'd enjoyed with Julian and what a real gentleman he was. In fact, so far he seemed to be the whole package.

What will she do if he has a girl back in London? She'd better watch out that she doesn't get too besotted in case he suddenly disappears back home. Ruby had real trouble getting out of her mind the way she felt with Julian's arm draped over her shoulders. She'd not made it obvious earlier in the day, but she wished it would never end— the body contact and unexpected intimacy.

Chapter Ten

Ruby woke to see Gamon waiting for her downstairs, eager to speak to her. 'You've done something I never thought could happen, my Ruby.'

'What's that Gammon, it sounds serious?'

'You forgot our appointment yesterday. We agreed to meet for afternoon tea and I wanted to discuss some issues that I wish to bring up at the meeting next week. I think we need to get you a proper diary.'

'I'm so sorry I doubled booked— and yes, you're right, I do need a diary of some kind.'

'I think I saw you looking very happy with our Julian walking up the driveway. What have you two been up to?'

'Nothing like that Gamon, we just had lunch together, that's all. We were discussing our relocation to the rural property,' said Ruby, hoping Gamon couldn't read her mind. 'It sounds as though it's going ahead.'

***

The move to the new rural premises in Rayong province was arduous. The team had plenty of helpers from the local community but moving from their temporary accommodation was daunting for the children. Some of them had been suffering from severe post-traumatic stress.

Ruby and Julian started unpacking the boxes.

'I feel so sorry for the residents having to go through all this change.'

'It's going to be much better for them in the long run. You know the saying short-term pain, long-term gain,' Julian replied.

'This building is far superior to our old one. Do you want me to contact the painters?' Ruby was keen to see the dated interior freshened up.

'No, don't worry, they're arriving next week. We made enough from the sale that we can completely renovate the building before the residents are transferred.'

'I can't wait to see their faces when they see their new rooms and the beautiful gardens here.' Ruby felt relieved that Rainbow Haven had been relocated away from Bangkok. She shuddered as she remembered how dark and sleazy parts of the city were. Not the right place for a rehabilitation centre, but it was the best her Mum and Dad could do with the funds they had at the time. How Ruby missed the country life—not long to go now.

Ruby and Julian sat under the weeping cherry tree on a wooden park bench that had been made from local hardwood branches. There was something nostalgic about it, and Ruby was trying to remember where she had seen a seat like that.

'That's a wooden seat like the one Mum and Dad have back home on the veranda at Peace Haven. I can even remember Belle and Milton, the founders, sitting on it in the evenings when we first went to live there.'

She started to feel a twinge of homesickness which she hadn't really felt until now. She'd been so involved with Rainbow Haven that she hadn't had time to think about home too much. Somehow the seat triggered something deep inside her.

She began to think of the whole community back at Peace Haven, especially the staff Annie and Murray who lived in Lavender Cottage. Annie had helped Ruby's mother, Cherie look after her when she was a baby, soon after her mother had been widowed.

Julian slipped his arm around Ruby's waist presumptuously, although there was no sign of reticence from Ruby who took the liberty of placing her hand over his. She relished the moment, as this was the first instance of any kind of real closeness with Julian since their lunch in the botanical gardens.

They both sat and watched the children roaming the park-like estate. The tropical flowers were in full bloom, as though they had put on a display of radiance to welcome the residents to their new home.

The ex-hotel was a colonial type building with long verandas and the new white paint on the exterior walls made the building appear like new.

There was a large tree hut in the garden which Julian had helped build. The children were overjoyed when they first saw it, especially the boys.

Gamon arrived with Isra in tow who followed her like a shadow. Gamon was four or five years older but had the wisdom of an old aunt rather than her university friend.

'This is amazing, isn't it? We've just arrived back from Phuket visiting my friends there. We've only been away three weeks and so much has been done here already! I'm feeling guilty about going on holiday at such a busy time.'

'It all went smoothly, Gamon. We had a big team helping us and you were well overdue for your holidays. You can't keep giving out if the bank is empty. You'll bankrupt your body.' Julian had such a kind tone that Ruby could get a glimpse of the man's heart, a soft heart.

***

Ruby had been to the Women's Aglow Christian fellowship meeting in Rayong twice now. She had to drive the Land Rover which was a communal vehicle that Rainbow Haven had at their disposal. The trip took just over an hour. There were a few ex-pats attending the meeting, but Ruby knew a few of the local Thai women who attended the meetings too. Gamon and Isra also accompanied Ruby.

She noticed an Australian woman with whom she had spoken at length the first time she went there. She had given a talk at that meeting about the orphanages she had set up in Pattaya and at the Cambodian border. Ruby remembers asking her a lot of questions. The woman told her she was pro-active in finding adoptive parents for the children in her orphanages and asked if there was a surplus at Rainbow Haven. She offered to take any overflow into her orphanage where they could be adopted out to rich Americans and Europeans if Rescue Net couldn't find the parents.

Ruby had felt there was something that just didn't sit right with this woman. She watched her interacting with one of the new arrivals at the meeting then approached her.

'Celia, how are you going with your orphanage?'

'Well, well. It's a surprise to see you after all this time. I thought you had returned home to Cromwell Mead by now.' The woman seemed to be pandering to Ruby, running off to fetch her refreshments and a plate of sandwiches.

Ruby mistrusted her, thinking she had a hidden agenda. 'My mother mentioned that you approached her about taking some of our children for adoption too.'

'Oh, that's right ... that was some time ago now. I could see Cherie and Lyon seemed stretched for space at one point when I visited and offered to help out.'

'Well thank you, but we appear to be managing quite well at present. We have moved the home to new premises, much bigger and well equipped than our previous one. I'm sure my parents will not want to move any of our children on, though I will mention it to them.'

Ruby's parents, though living back in Cromwell Mead on the other side of the world in New Zealand, were very protective of Rescue Net's safe house, Rainbow Haven, and made all the major decisions about the residents and the running of the home.

Later that evening, Ruby wandered out into the gardens, soaking up the strong sweet fragrance of the Ylang Ylang flowers. She loved good perfumes, so enjoyed any sweet-smelling flowers, which were plentiful in their new gardens.

As she wandered past the office, she saw the light was still on. It was Julian, still working. Ruby admired his dedication to his work at Rescue Net.

'Hey, you workaholic! It's time to knock off. What are you doing so late?' She stood in the doorway, wondering if she was sounding intrusive, while Julian sat looking intensely at what appeared to be a letter.

'Ruby! You made me jump. Are you in the habit of creeping up on people?' He gave her a friendly wink and put the kettle on. 'Stay for a cuppa before you turn in?'

'I'd love an Earl Grey tea thanks. There's something I'd like to run past you if you have time.'

'I'll always make time for you, Cherry Pie.'

Ruby was thrown off balance by this sudden expression of endearment from Julian. She'd never really formed any close intimate relationships with men. Most of her boyfriends turned out to be jerks, she kept telling her friends. She'd always been too guarded. She kept telling herself that she was afraid she'd end up with the wrong man as she'd seen too many of her friends in disastrous marriages.

But her feelings for this Englishman were deepening beyond her control. She wanted to move to another level, though she also knew that she must let it happen in God's time and not become another dismal statistic.

'Julian, I have met that woman again I told you about, the one with the orphanages. She approached me just like she approached my parents about getting some of our children adopted out.'

'That sounds a bit suspect to me. I can vaguely remember Lyon mentioning something about her some years ago.'

'She may have thought I would have some kind of power to make that decision, to over-ride my parents in some way. She seemed very manipulative.'

'We'll have to do a bit of research on her and her business I think. I'll see what I can do.' He started rinsing out their cups and placing them neatly back on the shelf.

Julian almost gave Ruby a hug before he turned out the light. It was as though he wanted to lean over and kiss her. Or was it just wishful thinking on Ruby's part.

'Don't you think it's time we went for another meal together? I'd like to take you out for dinner one evening, and I won't take no for an answer.'

'Sounds okay to me. But I do think it's my turn to shout you a meal.'

'I won't hear of it, Cherry Pie— anyway, I owe you for offering to iron my shirts when Kanda was away sick. You could have shown me how to iron them myself by the way. I also want to take you to the National Park, not far from here to check out the amazing waterfalls.'

Ruby climbed into bed that night wondering how all this was going to pan out. She prayed... 'Father, guide me and direct my path. Don't let self-will overwhelm me. Protect me from making wrong choices.'

As she prayed, sleep quickly consumed her.

Chapter eleven

Julian drove out to the countryside to visit Briggs Enterprises, a fish farm which had started using a new technology called aquaponics which he had never heard of. He was trying to drum up employment for some of the residents at Rainbow Haven.

As the Land Rover drove up the long driveway lined with flamboyant hibiscus trees to the farm manager's office, Julian was distracted by the professional looking set up in such a remote place.

Anton Briggs, the plant manager walked out to greet him. 'Good to finally meet you, Julian.' They shook hands. Julian had already spoken to him over the phone and detected a northern English accent.

'Come on in. I'll show you around and give you a rundown of how we operate. Can I offer you a drink, a beer, or fresh juice perhaps?'

'Thanks, juice would be fine.'

'Mia ... come and meet one of our new friends.'

Anton introduced Julian to his wife who appeared to be a mix of Thai and American.

'Mia runs all the administration side of things, thank goodness. I wouldn't have a clue how to do that side of things. I run the fish farm and I'll get you to meet Joe who manages the greenhouse. After you've had a good look around, we'll discuss the training program we can offer your residents.'

'Sure, thanks. I've had a good look at your magazine and find it very impressive. I'm sure it could work well for us and we have some very reliable and capable girls and lads who may be suited to this work.'

Julian spent the afternoon being shown around the plant and meeting all the staff. He felt a sense of excitement at the thought of the teenagers at Rainbow Haven being offered work in such an orderly environment. Anton and Mia were eager to get them into the program.

'I reckon we could come to a very satisfactory arrangement. We must talk again soon.'

'I need to discuss it with the directors and rest of the staff, then introduce the opportunity to the particular residents we have in mind for this training.'

As he drove back to Rayong enjoying the picturesque landscape, Julian chuckled as he watched a peasant farmer trying to coerce a few buffalo across the road through a gate. How advanced this country had become— how far it had progressed since he had first visited with his family fifteen years ago.

His thoughts wandered off onto his blossoming relationship with Ruby who had become a significant person in his life. Would she be feeling the same?

***

The next morning Ruby woke to the sound of loud squawking outside her window. She looked up at the bright yellow flowers of the Golden Shower tree, trying to spot the noisy culprits. They sounded like parrots. They were Macaws, giant parrots. She couldn't stop staring at their radiant red and green feathers. Then she saw a pair of cockatiel birds with head plumes that resembled British Household Cavalry hats. How free they appeared— free and unencumbered.

'Ruby, are you in there?'

She felt irritated that her special moment with nature had been interrupted.

'I need to talk to you.' Gamon was at her door and seemingly agitated, which was unlike her to be anything else but calm and unruffled.

'Come in, I'm just making breakfast. Have you eaten?' Ruby was about to make some French toast with banana and bacon on her primitive benchtop stove.

'Thanks, I've eaten, but I'd love a coffee if that's ok.'

'Sure, I've just made a fresh one. What's up?'

Gamon slid into a cane chair on the veranda.

'I've just had an interesting update about that woman who runs the orphanage. Remember you asked me to ask my friends if they anything about her?'

'Great, I sure do.'

'Well, I found out she also runs an adoption agency and has a lot of clients in America and Europe. It is supposed to be a non-profit making trust, a Christian charitable trust, so she says. But my friend Dao says that her clients are paying big money to the adoption agency.'

'That stinks. It sounds pretty suspect to me. Julian is also making inquiries about her. She seems to be quite defensive if you ask her questions about her business. I don't trust her.'

'I think she's using the orphanage as a front for the agency, and probably doesn't even try to find their real parents. Several children from the orphanage were picked up off the streets. The authorities don't want to know, as the problem is so big they can't deal with it, especially in Cambodia. They are only relieved that the children have found rich families to take over their care. It's privately run and funded by outsiders through donations.'

'When you've finished your coffee let's go and talk to Julian. He'll be most intrigued. He also has a few friends who work for social services who will be concerned about this.'

'Hold on, there's something else you may want to know.'

Gamon was obviously concerned that the Celia woman was some kind of fraud. She placed her hands over her flushed cheeks and let out a loud sigh. Ruby was unaccustomed to seeing her agitated like this.

She sat back down again so Gamon could tell her everything she knew.

'She seems to be a con artist Ruby, honestly. My friend Dao worked at that orphanage as a volunteer during the semester break. She loves children and was horrified at an incident she witnessed involving Celia. She said I could tell you in confidence but she doesn't want it to get back to that woman in case she retaliates.'

Ruby started to feel a chill run down her spine as she coaxed her friend into telling the truth about Celia.

'Dao was in the big nursery one day feeding the babies. There was a smaller room where a few infants were kept apart from the others, although she wasn't told why. That day, as she stood in the doorway of the room, she heard Celia harshly scolding a baby with nasty words.'

'What was she saying?'

'She was acting weird, saying something like "I'll teach you, nasty little devil. You horrible little creature if you think you can manipulate me!" She had a bottle of milk, poked the teat into her mouth, and as the baby started sucking, she pulled it away sharply. The child just couldn't stop screaming, she was so hungry. Dao said she felt sick, faint with the shock of witnessing such cruelty from the owner of an orphanage. The baby was only five months old.'

'That's horrific! She sounds like a sadist. It's a shame Dao didn't get a photo. The monster needs to be investigated more.' She looked at the ground, scuffing her shoe backwards and forwards then stopped.

'I know— I have a friend from Australia who has done some aid work and has worked at her orphanage. I thought it was a reputable place until now. I'll phone her and ask her what she thought of the woman.'

Julian was nowhere to be found. He must have gone into the village they thought. 'Don't worry Gamon. I'll have a talk to Julian and see how we can go about exposing her. If she is finding a loop-hole in the law, there's not a lot we can do but warn evangelical organisations about her.'

Gamon sloped off down the corridor with her arms hanging limply at her side and looking down at the ground.

Ruby's head ached. She was fed up with the corruption in these pseudo-evangelical organisations—especially in the poorer countries where the vulnerable were being exploited. Something has to be done about it. That woman needs to be exposed. Ruby was accustomed to blowing the whistle on corruption in so-called high places. Her parents had taught her well.

She felt weary as the day drew to a close. Once again she noticed the light on late in the office. Julian was sitting at his desk. What was he doing so late at night?

'Hi, there … mind if we catch up over a cuppa?' Ruby took the opportunity to find out what he was doing. 'I hope I'm not being intrusive, but I've noticed you've been in the office until rather late some nights. Is everything okay Julian—I mean— are you in some kind of trouble?'

'Oh, sorry Ruby, I wasn't aware you were concerned. I was trying to avoid telling you that something has come up that I need to deal with and I've been holding off from telling anyone until I was sure.'

'What do you mean? Sorry, I don't understand.'

'It's my Mum in London, she's very ill and my brother has been keeping me informed about when to fly home.'

Ruby felt a jolt go through her. Was she suddenly going to lose this lovely man she had come to know and trust so well? She felt ashamed of her self-concern and quickly directed her attention to the aggrieved Julian.

'I'm so sorry Julian. Has she been ill for long?'

'No, she had a severe stroke a month ago and has not recovered that well. There has also been a clot in a blood vessel to her heart that is causing more problems. It's touch-and-go whether she sees the year out.'

'Why didn't you tell any of us? We could have offered you support.'

'I wanted to make sure the move from Bangkok to Rayong went smoothly for the children. It would have caused a huge disruption if I had flown to London then.'

Ruby admired his compassion and sense of loyalty even more.

'Ruby, I'm going to have to go over there in a day or two, but I need to let your folks know once I've booked, as Lyon will come out and relieve me for a while until I can get back here again.'

Julian walked her to her room and told her all about his trip to the aquaponics farm and the training program which her parents had asked him to follow up.

'Where has your mother been living—in a rest home for the elderly or in her own home?'

'With my brother Larry in the Bed and Breakfast hotel called The Gables. My parents bought the business when we all left home, then after Dad died Larry took it over. I was still at university. He and his wife, Maggie have helped Mum to run the business until she recently took ill.'

Ruby was worried that Julian would be expected to stay back and work at the hotel. What will she do if he never comes back?

'I suppose you have enough on your plate now without hearing about that Celia woman from the orphanages. Gamon has been with me today, very eager to update me about the fraudster.'

'I tell you what. Why don't you let me take you out to dinner tomorrow night to that Irish pub I was telling you about—the one that has live music playing? You can tell me all about it there.'

Julian leaned over, taking the liberty of kissing her on the cheek, hesitated, then walked off. Ruby relished the moment again and silently prayed .... Please, God, don't let him disappear out of my life, not now, please.

As she lay in bed listening to the autumn rain falling delicately on the tin roof, she felt there was something special happening between herself and Julian. Their friendship had grown into something more meaningful. She hoped that whatever circumstances put a distance between them, Julian would always find her ... or would he? She tried hard not to let it trouble her. Perhaps she should come right out and tell him how she feels.

The rain on the roof soothed her into a deep sleep.

***

The four teenage girls and an adolescent boy who signed up for the aquaponics training program were transported to the farm at the end of the week by Julian and another staff member and Gamon accompanied the girls. The residents were so excited at the chance of paid employment at the end of it.

Ruby stayed back to check her mail. She remembered having received several newsletters from Celia the last few months which she had just filed away without reading them. She picked up the pile and started perusing them. She was particularly interested in the bank account details at the bottom of them. There were three bank accounts, but none of them was a trust account and they all had her own name assigned to them. They appeared to be her personal accounts but Ruby had no proof. Celia also had reference to her adoption agency which seemed inappropriate. The last time Ruby met her in public was at the weekly market where she was shopping with Gamon. She had felt something just didn't sit right. Celia had swanned her way through the crowd with her head in the air, flamboyantly overdressed in what appeared to be expensive clothes, especially for Thailand where clothes are so cheap.

Ruby began to smell a rat. She could see that this woman's life appeared to be a huge contradiction, under the guise of working to save orphans and finding them good homes with wealthy people. Ruby read Celia's old newsletters now in a more detailed manner. There were some articles from rich Americans and Europeans who were funding her, mostly people who had adopted a child and continued to support Celia financially.

The hypocrisy made Ruby's blood boil. She must talk to Julian to see what can be done to expose her.

Chapter Twelve

Julian appeared immaculately dressed in navy blue Chino trousers, white polo shirt, and shiny brown leather shoes. Ruby was once again impressed with his dress sense.

'Are you ready? Sorry— I know I'm a bit early—it might be difficult to get a car park today. It's one of their busiest days. Thanks for making it.' Julian looped arms with her as they wandered out to the Land Rover.

He had promised to take her to Rayong's popular seafood restaurant on the wharf and this week they had huge king prawns on the menu, her favourite. She sat next to him constantly twisting the dress ring on her middle finger, wondering what he wanted to say to her and was eager to get there to listen to him.

'I'm paying and you can have the run of the menu and no argument.' He leaned over and squeezed her hand.

The restaurant had a pleasant, relaxed ambience and to Ruby's relief, the easy-listening music emanating from the speakers above her was that of Burt Bacharach. It was a change from the usual traditional Thai music played at their local restaurants.

They ordered a pineapple and jackfruit cocktail with crushed ice, refreshing on humid days such as this. Julian was generously wanting Ruby to enjoy the run of the menu. He appeared awkward, as though he was bursting to say something then kept holding back. Finally, he spouted forth—'Ruby, my mother has got worse ... I'm going to have to fly out this weekend. Larry is picking me up from Heathrow on Saturday night and I'll be staying at The Gables until the worst is over. Your father is coming over to stay until I can get back.' He leaned over the table, gently stroking her fingers. Ruby felt confused about this display of affection, especially when he was about to leave for an unknown period of time. She knew she just had to trust that he would be back, but she didn't want to upset herself and quickly changed the subject.

She told him all the news about Celia and Julian said he had been receiving her newsletters too. He had met her a year ago at some missions evening where she was giving a talk about her orphanages, trying to drum up business from unsuspecting church people.

'Look, I have a plan. I know someone, in fact, a good friend of mine called Phillipe from Manilla in the Philippines. He is in the Rayong police force. He's been with Rescue Net on most of the raids. His speciality is cyber-crime and he may know a way that this Celia woman can be found to be in breach of some law. Especially regarding a conflict of interest with the orphanage and adoption agency. He gets really vocal about the exploitation of children. I'll call him tomorrow and have a long talk about it. He can keep in touch with you while I'm away and I can phone him if need be.'

***

A month had passed and Ruby had been upset thinking that Julian may have changed his mind and decided to stay and help his brother at The Gables. Her father was a great support as usual and had such superb management skills that it was so easy to let him run the place.

'Your mother misses you, Ruby, quite a lot actually but won't let on,' said Lyon. 'But she knows you've been a vital part of the running of the centre and the relocation.'

'I know, I miss everybody too, in fact, I've been feeling quite homesick this past month.'

'Mmm … Are you sure you aren't pining for somebody I know?'

'You mean Julian! Don't be ridiculous, we aren't an item, not that I know about anyway. We are just friends.' Ruby hoped that her lack of self-honestly over her feelings for Julian would not be easily detected by her father, who knew her well.

'He promised he would be back, as Rainbow Haven can't really manage without him for too long.' Ruby tried to sound unemotional.

She continued …'I don't think anyone should make promises, as we're not in control of our lives. Regardless, he told me he would be back.'

Lyon tugged on her arm. 'Come on—let's go and pick up the crew from Briggs farm. I'd like to have a good look around too, so we'd better get out there a bit earlier.'

As usual, Mia was a warm and hospitable hostess when she met Lyon. Joined by Anton, they sat discussing the progress of Rainbow Haven's residents and the possibility of work for them all once their training was over.

'We've been expanding a great deal this year so the extra staff will be good,' said Anton.

Lyon noticed that Ruby was far away, distracted rather than bored. She was trying to decide how long she would want to wait in Thailand for Julian to return. She really was quite homesick although she was devoted to the care and welfare of the residents of Rainbow Haven. She was torn between staying on there and returning home. But her relationship with Julian had now added another whole dimension to her dilemma.

'Are you still with us Ruby?' Mia observed her detachment while offering her another curry puff.

'Oh, sorry! I was miles away... I've had a lot on my plate lately. Please excuse me.' Her face reddened.

'Come on, Ruby, I think we need to get our crew loaded into the van and get back. Thanks, both of you for the guided tour. You have an impressive business going here and it's great to see the smiles on the faces of our young people since they've been in your program. We're very grateful you have offered them this opportunity.'

'You're welcome … we're enjoying them too and they are hard workers. They'll make you proud, you wait and see.'

As the van pulled into the driveway at Rainbow Haven, Lani the cook came out to meet them. Tuesdays they brought home fresh fish from Brigg's fish farm, a charitable gift from the Briggs to the trainees. Some of the residents were trained in culinary arts and looked forward to trying their hand at presenting the community at Rainbow Haven with an exotic fish dish.

After the meal, Ruby sat on a wooden bench under the bright red Flame Tree. This was her favourite resting place. She was mesmerised by the subtle shades of pink and orange of a tropical sunset. Heartfelt memories of the time her mother used to read to her from the Bible flooded her mind. Her mother often told her about rainbow promises. Ruby had been told by children and teachers that there was a pot of gold at the end of the rainbow which she had always believed until her mother told her the truth. She told her that God gave the rainbow as a promise that he is faithful to us and we can trust him.

She began to think of all the false promises that were made to her, promises that were broken, starting with her ex-fiancée Richard. She had even made promises to friends she couldn't keep. That must be the "false gold" or "fool's gold" at the end of the rainbow. But God's promises are never empty—he always comes through. That's why Rainbow Haven is a great name for a safe house where broken people need hope. It was aptly named by her mother.

'There you are, I was wondering where you had got to. Is everything alright Ruby?'

'I was just doing some meditation. I'm fine thanks.'

Ruby felt uncomfortable with suddenly being put on the spot, even by her father. She had always tried to be strong and resilient like her mother had been, especially having survived her late husband's narcissism. Her mother's strong determination had rubbed off on Ruby, but somehow, Julian's absence had started to cause a chink in her armour.

'I thought you might like to have an update about that woman who runs the adoption agency in Pattaya. I've had a phone call from Julian's friend Phillipe. Apparently what she is doing on the surface appears legitimate, but she has cleverly found a legal loophole to be able to sell her orphan babies for profit. Phillipe has a lawyer friend who subsequently carried out further investigations and found a way to deter her from continuing the adoption agency for profit. She has been receiving government funding and the authorities will allow her to carry on adopting out the children, but she is now unable to charge the exorbitant fees to the new parents. She can only charge enough to cover minor administrative costs.'

'Wow! That's fantastic Dad, good old Phillipe. I'll bet Julian will be over the moon to hear the news. I hope Celia doesn't connect it to me in any way.'

'No, why should she? It has all been carried out in a highly confidential manner as all police work is. You stop worrying, my girl.'

'Are you going to get in touch with Julian to let him know?' Ruby said with an almost pleading tone.

'I'll do that for you, just chill out,' said Lyon, making it obvious he had read her mind, leaving her beaming from ear to ear.

The next morning Ruby knocked on her father's bedroom door in the coordinator's flat where Julian usually resided.

'Coming in for a coffee? What's up, Ruby?' Lyon had been up early preparing the documents and reports the police had requested for an impending raid they planned on a hotel-brothel in Pattaya.

'I was just wondering ... when do you plan to phone Julian?' Suddenly she felt exposed.

'I was going to phone this morning, but I checked the diary and our next big raid is tomorrow. I need to spend some time organising it. Look, Ruby, I think it best if I just wait until after the raid—then I can let him know the outcome of that too. If his mother is so ill, it's best to just keep it simple and stick to the things that directly affect Rescue Net at present.'

After Lyon had spoken, he wondered if he had spoken too soon when he looked at the dejected look on Ruby's face.

'Tell you what ... you drop Julian a line with all the update on Rainbow Haven—such as the trainees' involvement with Briggs farm? You can let him know about the outcome with the adoption agency and what Phillipe is doing. He may give you some indication when he's coming back then, but don't pressurise him.' Ruby's face lit up like a child being given an ice-cream.

She went back inside and carried a basket full of ripe, tropical passion fruit around to the main kitchen. For days now, she had been wondering how she was going to use the fruit to give the residents a treat. Though the culinary students did most of the cooking, the rest of the staff took turns helping out in the kitchen. She decided to make an ice-cream dessert using her own green tea ice-cream with fresh pineapple from Rainbow Haven's trees, and the passionfruit.

As she busied herself cutting up the fruit, she looked out the window and saw Gamon walking in the garden in deep conversation with the Youth Worker, Rolando, who was half Thai, half Canadian. He had been on the staff for several years, but Ruby hadn't noticed that he and Gamon were such good friends and something was in the air, like a new romance.

Chapter Thirteen

A few weeks had gone by and there had been no reply from Ruby's letter to Julian. She couldn't understand what was going on, as she was very careful not to make any demands or sound needy in her letter. She wrote it in a general way, just keeping him up to date with the events at Rescue Net.

She lay in bed thinking he must have changed his mind about returning to Rainbow Haven. His family may have talked him into staying to help run The Gables, or perhaps because his mother had died he was too upset to think of anything else. Disappointed, Ruby lay there thinking it may be time for her to return home to Cromwell Mead, as the staff at Rainbow Haven were now able to manage the running of the centre now, and her father could employ someone else to take Julian's place.

It wasn't her decision to make, seeing she had just been there to help out. She tried to block out the sound of the locusts which rallied on hot dry nights under her window and started thinking about her future.

Suddenly she felt alone and wondered if there would ever be anyone special in her life again. She was even more downhearted at the thought of never seeing lovely Julian again and having no one special to spend Christmas with. Sleep came quickly to her.

Rainbow Haven was a hive of enthusiastic activity at Christmas with many of the children helping the staff with Christmas decorations. For some of them, it meant nothing more than a festive occasion of fun, good food and recreation. For others like Gamon, Isra and another small group of Christian followers, it was a special occasion and they met with their little church group.

'Come on, Gamon, we'll be late for our staff meeting,' said Ruby, calling her friend who was hanging out her washing. Dad has something he wants to tell us all together, hurry!' Ruby waited for her friend to catch up.

'Tell me, Ruby, you must know what's going on?' They walked towards the meeting room.

'I honestly haven't a clue. He doesn't always tell me everything.'

Lyon began, 'Thank you all for coming today. I know its short notice, but there are a few items of urgency I need to discuss with you. First of all, as you know, your coordinator, Julian, was called away to attend his sick mother. Well, I have just had word that she has passed away and her funeral was a few days ago. He said he needs to stay on for a bit longer to help his brother settle her affairs, so I will be staying on here until he gets back if you can all put up with me.' He turned and winked at Ruby.

'Secondly— Cherie and I have elected another senior staff member to manage the male residence. You all know Rolando our Youth worker who is more than qualified for the task. He has accepted the position as supervisor, which is a management role. Rolando's background with Child Development and Welfare in Pattaya has placed him as an esteemed team member at Rescue Net. Gamon will remain supervisor of the girl's residence and their programs along with Trudy our nurse who lives off-site.'

Ruby just sat there, unable to focus on the rest of Lyon's agenda. She couldn't understand why Julian had written to her father, instead of replying to her own letter. Was he avoiding her, and if so, why? She was relieved she hadn't exposed her true feelings to him. Now she'll be careful not to betray herself by exposing her true feelings about Julian to her father either, no matter how caring and respectful he is. She had her heart broken once with her first love, and she wasn't going to get hurt like that again. Not if she can help it.

'Ruby, can you give me a hand to put the whiteboard and things away?' asked Lyon.

The meeting had ended and the residents were in the tearoom having their afternoon tea. Lyon noticed Ruby's despondency.

'Come on, Ruby, what's up, you seem to be so distant lately?' Lyon wasn't used to her being so subdued, as she was usually bright and cheerful. 'Hold on ... did you end up writing to Julian? I forgot to ask you how you got on.' He sensed there was some unfinished business over that issue. 'You never mentioned it, that's all.'

Ruby froze—she felt cornered and knew she couldn't lie about what had happened. She explained to her father the contents of her letter and that she just couldn't work Julian out. Then to hear the news second-hand from her father about Julian's mother and his change of plans ...

'Oh, Dad, I thought we had become so close, at least that was the impression he was giving me. Now he appears to be avoiding me.' Ruby's voice quavered.

'Look, Ruby, I don't think it's anything of the sort. I think he was too emotional over the death of his mother, and as a man, I can understand that if he starts writing to you right now while he is in a vulnerable state, he might open himself up too quickly. I think you'll hear from him when it all settles down, trust me.'

Ruby appreciated the reassurance of Lyon but still couldn't believe that Julian was still interested in her.

'Why don't you send him a condolence card, Ruby?'

'I was thinking about it then my hurt pride stopped me.'

Lyon handed Ruby the letter he had received from Phillipe outlining the outcome of the saga with Celia and her adoption agency.

'There you are— she won't be making a profit from poor orphans anymore. She won't like having to run the orphanage as a non-for-profit organisation without the adoption agency to prop up her flamboyant lifestyle.'

'Well, I don't know how the authorities have let her get away with it all this time, beats me! She must know someone high up, I'll bet, someone she could manipulate.'

***

Christmas was almost around the corner. Those who traditionally celebrated Christmas busied themselves making handmade gifts for the other residents. The centre always received parcels from the charities that supported them. Ruby began thinking how cosy it would be if she could spend Christmas with Julian, but it looked like it wasn't going to happen. Lyon wanted to get back home to spend it with Cherie he had told Ruby.

Two weeks before Christmas, Ruby was busy in her pantry about to put bread into the new toaster Lyon had bought her. She always had toast with her coffee for breakfast. She wasn't a morning person and found it a chore having to turn up in the dining room downstairs before nine each morning so she always ate in her room.

She woke to find her father calling to her from under her balcony. 'Can you come down soon? I've something for you that might put a smile on your face. I'll wait for you down here while I'm hosing the garden.'

Ruby felt intrigued. What did he have up his sleeve?

Lyon had always been more than a father to her after he had married her mother. He had adopted her when she was an adolescent and she was grateful that she had not grown up with her psychotic biological father. Lyon Preston had always treated Ruby as his own daughter.

She finished her coffee and toast and wandered into the garden. When Lyon saw her coming, he dropped the hose and slipped his hand inside his jacket to fetch a packet. What was he up to, Ruby wondered?

'Ruby, someone has given me this to give to you. It's meant to be your Christmas present but they asked me to give it to you now, a special request.'

'Who is it from? I'll bet it's a voucher or something. I can't think who would do that, as I don't know anyone well enough over here. Anyway, friends of mine would give it to me personally.'

'Come on girl, aren't you going to open it?' Lyon couldn't wait to see her reaction.

Inside the brown paper packet was a dainty pink gift bag with something inside it. Ruby, still expecting a gift voucher, stared in disbelief when an air ticket for Qantas airlines popped out. She glanced rapidly at the details and saw her name was on the ticket and the flight to London was four days before Christmas.

'What's this— did you do this Dad?'

'No, it wasn't me. Look inside the bag again.'

She pulled out a card with a purple butterfly covered in glitter and a note inside the card. To her surprise, she saw that it was from Julian ....

Hi Ruby

I hope you don't find this presumptuous, but I wanted to give you a big surprise this Christmas. I did get your letter but I was in a quandary as to what to do when my mother was dying. I didn't want to commit to coming back at the time, as I was under pressure to help my brother Larry and felt confused and torn. I stayed in contact with your father who kept me up to date with Rescue Net and other things. Larry needs help tying up my mother's estate at The Gables in Devon transferring the ownership deeds into the family Trust as he continues to run the lodge. Once that's all over, I can return to Thailand.

I've really missed you and have been afraid someone may whisk you off your feet while I'm away. A wee bird told me that you had been asking about me too.

Ruby, it would give me great pleasure if you would spend Christmas here in Devon with me and perhaps stay on a little longer then we can return to Rainbow Haven together. Lyon has said that he has a plan worked out for staffing at Rainbow Haven during this time. What do you think? I'd be so disappointed if you turned me down, but I understand it's taken you by surprise.

I would so much love to show you my beautiful hometown, Cheriton Bishop. That's where I grew up when my parents were raising calves. There are some amazing walks here around our village and we make the best apple cider in all of Devon. You must bring your camera.

I do hope you'll accept the return ticket. It's my Christmas gift to you and I am so looking forward to seeing you. Larry and Maggie are eager to meet you.

Your dearest friend and secret admirer from afar

Julian

Chapter Fourteen

Ruby was blown away with the tickets and more so with Julian's confession. She didn't know whether to laugh or cry and felt overwhelmed after all the tension of the past three weeks since he had left. Especially when she'd received no response to her letter.

'Well, what do you think love?' Lyon felt so relieved to see Ruby looking happy for once, as she'd been so downcast lately. She lunged at him and gave him such a tight squeeze that he almost lost his breath. She was still in disbelief.

'But how can I go and leave you alone over Christmas to manage on your own? You were going home to join Mum for Christmas, weren't you? How can you leave now if Julian and I won't be here?'

'Don't you worry about that. We have it all sorted.'

'Who's we? What do you mean?'

'Your mother is coming out here for Christmas and will stay until you and Julian get back. You'll see her before you fly out. Peace Haven will be closed for a month and we have organised some relieving managers who we usually use to fill in while we're away.'

Ruby felt this sudden turn-around in her life was overwhelming and needed to get her head around it. She also realised how much she had taken her father for granted, as he was always so caring and protective of her.

She sat at her desk trying to ward off the butterflies in her stomach as she prepared to write to Julian and tell him the news about her impending arrival. The tickets were flexible, and her father helped her book her flights to London.

Hi Julian

First of all, I'm so sorry to hear the sad news about your mother. It must have been difficult for you going home to find her in that state. It's good your brother has you to help him through it all.

You've no idea how overwhelmed I was to receive your amazing gift. And yes, I am coming tout suite! I've really missed your company, to be perfectly honest, and when I didn't hear from you, I thought I'd never see you again.

I'm so looking forward to seeing Cheriton Bishop and going on those walks with you. I've been looking at pictures of your village in a book I got out of the library. It looks so beautiful. Especially the quaint narrow lanes with hedgerows and the houses with thatched rooves just as you described.

I'll send you my flight booking. Dad said you are able to pick me up from Heathrow Airport. My mother is arriving soon so it will be great to spend some time with her for a few days before I fly out.

I so look forward to coming.
God Bless

Ruby

Chapter Fifteen

Cherie met Lyon and Ruby in the arrival lounge of the airport. 'Mum, give me a big hug! I've missed you heaps.' Ruby held her mother longer than usual, inhaling a deep whiff of Cherie's familiar Red Door perfume.

Ruby took one of her bags while Lyon pushed her luggage trolley over to the car. Cherie and Lyon sat chatting away in the front catching up, while Ruby sat in the back daydreaming about life in Devon. Cherie started discussing life back at Peace Haven, Ruby's childhood home. Belle and Milton, the founders of Peace Haven were still living out their senior years at their home, Seabird Lodge, and visiting Peace Haven, though Cherie thought they would be better off in a retirement village as they were very old and frail. Ruby always had such fond thoughts of Belle and Milton, especially Belle who gave Cherie enormous support when Ruby's father died.

The other Directors, Annie, and Murray were getting on in years too, but still remained in Lavender Cottage and were employed part-time. They often asked about Ruby as Annie was like a nanny to her when she and her mother moved into Peace Haven. Ruby had very fond thoughts of all the staff at the retreat as they had been like family to her, an extended family.

'Hey Ruby, are you still with us? You're very quiet.' Lyon turned around to check her out. He suspected she was daydreaming about her trip to England. 'Time to come off cloud ten, girl.' Cherie turned around and gave her a warm smile, as though she could read her thoughts.

The next day, Ruby took Gamon and Isra to the Christmas market in Rayong. The girls wanted to help her choose some clothes to take to England. There were only a couple of stalls that sold suitable clothing for cold weather and Ruby hadn't brought anything like that to Thailand.

'Look at this one, Ruby.' Isra held up a stylish cobalt blue, merino cape.

'It's difficult to know what it looks like without a mirror. That blue is one of my favourite colours, but I'm annoyed I can't try it on first before buying'.

'Trust us, Ruby, you'll look so elegant in that, just gorgeous, honestly!'

'Ok, thanks, both of you'. She bartered with the seller and managed to get it at a reasonable price. It wasn't as expensive as it looked.

'Just a couple of jumpers and some warm trousers now. I can't see any here—let's go a few blocks down. I think I know a place.' Ruby looped arms with the girls and led the way.

They arrived back at Rainbow Haven with a carload of shopping bags, mostly for Ruby. She knew she was going to miss both of these friends with whom she had formed a close alliance. Her life was so full of changes.

***

Julian kept looking at the overhead digital billboard to check the flight arrival. He tugged at his fringe trying to sweep it out of his eyes while he nervously waited in the arrival lounge. Perhaps she had changed her mind. Then he caught sight of a stunning figure of a woman dressed in what looked like a cobalt blue cape with stylish, denim jeans and brown boots. She must have dressed for the snow drift that had arrived the day before she flew out. He waved, grinning from ear to ear.

Ruby wanted to throw herself into Julian's arms, but she controlled herself, not wanting to scare him. She had waited so long for this day and it had finally arrived. Instead, Julian rushed up, wrapped his arms around her, and squeezed her so hard that she had to catch her breath. She kept looking at him, how suave he appeared. She quickly scanned him from head to toe. He wore brown leather Brogue shoes, black tee shirt, thick brown Bomber jacket with fleecy collar and tan corduroy trousers. A complete change of wardrobe from how he dressed in tropical Thailand.

Julian continued to be the gentleman he was, taking her luggage off the baggage carousel and placing it on the trolley.

'Off we go ... you carry your hand luggage Ruby and I'll push this. My car is parked outside. I hope you're hungry as Mrs Douglas has something special for you tonight.'

Ruby felt a cold blast hit her outside the front entrance of the terminal that took her by surprise, especially after boarding the aircraft in thirty degrees temperatures and arriving in London in three degrees, knocking her flat.

Julian had organised for the two of them to stay the night with Mrs Douglas, an elderly widow with whom Julian had boarded when he was at university. He wanted to surprise Ruby with a guided tour of London the next day, prior to travelling to Devon in the South West.

'Nice to meet you, Ruby, you must be hungry. I hope you like roast beef and Yorkshire pudding?' Mrs D, a buxom woman who looked more like a farmer's wife than a city slicker, warmly kissed Ruby on the cheek and placed her cape on a hanger.

'I have sticky date pudding with custard and cream to warm you up afterwards,' she said warmly.

Ruby was hungry, even though she had eaten a small meal on the plane. She guessed it was the excitement and adrenaline rush with the build-up to meeting Julian.

'I hope you've brought some warm clothes, my girl. The weather forecast predicts snow is on its way,' said Mrs D, as she meticulously set the table with her best bone china. 'Especially in Devon.'

'Yes, thanks. I picked up some things at the markets in Thailand before I left.' Ruby could see that Mrs D was the motherly sort, enjoying clucking over her. Her stately multi-level Victorian home near Sloane Square had been home to many university students, including Julian for a while.

Mrs D showed them their rooms. She made sure she put Ruby downstairs near her room and told Julian he was on the next floor. Julian remembers her telling him that she didn't run a "knocking shop" when he first met her.

Ruby had rested for an hour after lunch. She woke and dressed in warmer clothes then wandered into the living room. Julian was waiting for her eager to show her the sights.

'Come on Ruby, let's go into Sloane Square. I want to take you to one of my favourite places I used to go to during my student days.' Ruby grabbed her blue cape which Julian wrapped around her shoulders. She'd made sure she had plenty of thermals under her woollen top when Mrs D warned them that a big freeze was coming.

'Here we are ... pity we've had a late lunch, as they do some amazing hot pots here.

The Duke of Wellington, or the Wellington Boot as it was known, was a popular London pub that Julian and his colleagues dined in regularly.

Ruby was wondering why Julian was so fascinated with this pub, seeing he didn't drink much and nor did she. He ordered a Guinness and non-alcoholic cider for Ruby.

'I don't know how you can drink that awful black stuff!' she said, screwing up her face. 'That's stout, isn't it? Dad likes that too.'

'That's because he knows it's good for him. It's full of iron.' He put his drink down, showed Ruby to a comfortable armchair by the glowing fireplace, and walked over towards the elaborate piano in the corner.

Julian took a seat at the piano and to Ruby's astonishment, his hands started to flow gently over the keys from which emanated the most beautiful music. The melody startled Ruby. He was playing and singing one of her favourite songs – "The Look of Love" by Diana Krall. Then she noticed he kept looking back at her adoringly while he played. She didn't know whether to feel embarrassed or elated, though she was thinking he must really be quite smitten with her. How sweet. Is that why he brought me all the way over here? I'm sure he meant the words of the song to convey a message to me.

It was late afternoon. More customers gathered around the piano with their requests which he played with ease. Ruby realised that this was what attracted him to this pub.

'Talented, isn't he?' Said an older man and his wife who sat next to her.

'We have been coming here every week on a Friday night to hear Julian play,' he continued. 'And it's a wonder he isn't married, as he's such a kind person and will do anything for anyone,' said his wife.

'And you are new here, aren't you? What do you think of Julian's music? Isn't he a darling?' The woman seemed a little obsessed with him, Ruby thought.

'Ah ... yes, it's lovely. Actually, we are friends and colleagues. We have been working together in Thailand doing charity work.'

'Oh, that sounds lovely. He must be fun to work with.'

'Yes he is, he's quite a clever man.' Ruby decided to hold back and not to let on too much, as it was early days for them both.

Julian stood up and one of his acquaintances walked over to give him ginger and pineapple juice, one of his usual orders if he is not drinking Guinness.

He approached Ruby. 'Well ... what did you think? Thought I'd surprise you. I've been wanting to do this for a long time. I hope you don't mind!'

'Mind? Don't be silly— you never told me you were such an entertainer and play the piano so well. You have such an amazing voice too. You really are a dark horse, Julian. It sounds like you've had a lot of experience entertaining like this?'

'I started doing it at university in my bohemian days when I hung out with students at this pub. I started tinkering a bit on this piano when I was asked if I would play on a Friday night. One day I started singing as I played, and it went from there. They paid me handsomely which helped me pay my rent.'

Ruby was quite taken aback by it all. She gathered he had also played "The Look of Love" for her benefit and wasn't sure how to take it. She wasn't keen to jump into relationships, although she had known Julian for quite some time now and was completely taken by him. Still, she thought, what would it hurt to let things progress slowly and see how it pans out? After all, she'd already fallen in love with him.

Chapter Sixteen

The next day Julian took her on a guided tour of London and there was so much to see. They went riding on the big double-decker bus that toured the city including Buckingham Palace and Westminster Cathedral. That was a highlight for Ruby. They jumped off the bus at Hyde Park where there was someone giving a speech at Speaker's Corner.

'Come on Ruby, follow me. I'm going to show you some amazing paintings along Bayswater Road.'

They wandered past display upon display for what seemed miles, to Ruby.

'Mmm, I smell something tasty, there must be a food stall nearby,' she said, hoping they could stop and eat, having had enough of sight-seeing for the day.

'You're right, look over there. That's the local food market they have here every Saturday.' Julian ran over and purchased two giant lamb kebabs and a couple of berry smoothies. 'Here we are, just for us,' he said, pointing to a park bench under a huge oak tree.

***

Mrs D sat talking to them both, sitting in front of a roaring fire in the living room. 'Well, my dear, what do you think of London? What did you like most from the tour today?'

'I reckon Madam Tussauds was amazing, I've never seen anything like it. They all look so real.'

'But that wasn't to compare with the piano recital yesterday, now was it? I thought that would have grabbed you more!' said Julian, grinning at Mrs D who already knew that Julian had planned to surprise Ruby that evening. Ruby blushed and got out of her chair then slipped upstairs to the bathroom, while Mrs D took the opportunity to give Julian her opinion of his new girlfriend.

'She's such a likeable girl, Julian you'd better make sure you keep hold of this one. She's one in a million, that girl is.'

'I was a bit worried she might have someone waiting for her back home, but I don't think she has. I'm sure she is quite smitten with me.'

'Are you going back to Thailand with her?'

'Not yet. I need to go down to Devon to help sort out my mother's estate with my brother, then I'll have to get back to relieve Ruby's parents at Rainbow Haven so they can return home.'

'Well, you know you are welcome to bring her back here anytime. I can see myself growing very fond of the lass.'

The next morning Julian took Ruby shopping for Christmas gifts for his family. He wanted to see the look on her face when he took her for a stroll through famous Harrod's store.

As they wandered through Knightsbridge, there in front of her stood the most amazing store she had ever seen. Ruby was mesmerised as though she had just walked into a fairyland. The whole street was completely lit up with elaborate Christmas decorations that she had never seen before. Such extravagance she thought, but for now, she would enjoy being a passive spectator of London's rich and famous. Harrods was delightfully lit up and full of colour. Their display was spectacular. As they strolled outside the front of the store, there in front of them was an awesome sight. A huge display of Swarovski figures that appeared to be depicting a scene from Dickens with trees of ice and snow all made from the crystal. It was magical.

'Let's go inside—I'll buy you coffee and cake at the posh cafe. 'Julian put his arm around her waist proudly. As they sat and ate their authentic Eccles cakes and drank their latte coffees Ruby couldn't help thinking of the huge contrast between the lifestyle they just left behind in Thailand. She almost felt guilty but justified it by saying to herself that this was an education, which it was, and that she was just an onlooker. She had never in her life seen such extravagant materialism. So this is how the so-called privileged life, she pondered.

As they descended on the escalator, she was constantly pushed and shoved by people in expensive fur coats and hats, carrying armfuls of extravagantly wrapped parcels with gold ribbons. They oozed wealth.

Julian took her hand as he could see the disorientated look on her innocent face. 'Come with me, quick, we'll jump on that bus over there!'

Jump they certainly had to, as it was about to take off. They clambered on the back, holding the railing tight. The conductress took their money. 'Two to Oxford Street thanks,' said Julian.

Ruby observed how confident Julian was getting around London where he had spent most of his adult years once he had left home.

Ruby, on the other hand, felt lost in the crowd—completely unaccustomed to huge crowds after living in the small town of Cromwell Mead.

'Where are you taking me now?' She asked.

'I want to show you another store like Harrods. This one you may have seen in the movies.'

Ruby was trying to work out which one that was.

They arrived in Oxford Street and there it was, just as they stepped off the bus - SELFRIDGES. Dazzled by the lights, she tried to look upwards to see what else was on the sign. It said "CHRISTMAS" in dazzling coloured lights. This store was another sight to behold, but not if one was poor and needy like some of the homeless they passed as they wandered along the street.

Julian had told her not to give them money. Instead, he said to buy them some food so they won't be able to waste the money on drugs or alcohol. He had worked with the homeless in London and knew the drill well. As they passed a row of them near Oxford Circus, he stepped into MacDonald's and ordered a huge beef burger and hot chocolate. He took Ruby's hand again and led her out to the pavement, handing the burger and drink to an old man who appeared cold and hungry. He had a white beard and could almost be taken for Santa Claus, Ruby thought.

He could be someone's father, so heart-breaking. Ruby peered at the old man's sad eyes, and the look of gratitude was heart-rending for her. They walked away, both whispering silently to themselves that it never felt enough— it would never be enough.

'Don't the social services come and round them up and take them to a shelter? There are so many of them.' Ruby was unaccustomed to seeing such destitution in wealthy westernised cities. She knew it existed in South East Asia, but this was unfathomable for her where she came from.

'Many of these people choose to stay on the streets. I've done a lot of work with them and some of them know me. They will tell you they want to be free of the pressures of society such as laws, rules, and regulations which is complete freedom in their eyes. But they just can't grasp that they are really in bondage this way.'

Ruby felt powerless, and being a compulsive rescuer like her mother by nature, she just couldn't cope. 'Can we go back now?'

***

The train to Devon was leaving early the next morning. Ruby sensed that snow could be in the air and was relieved

98

she had worn thermals under her clothing. She even bought herself a thick winter coat from an upmarket recycle boutique.

'Hey Rubes, we'd better get a move on to Platform Two. It leaves in ten minutes.' Julian started gaining momentum, struggling along the platform with an oversized suitcase.

Ruby loved taking the train. This reminded her of the long trip she took with Kate in Australia to Bonalbo. She realised she hadn't been in touch with her friend for a while and must get back and drop her a line. Suddenly she caught sight of a herd of wild ponies. 'Look at them, aren't they beautiful? Are they all wild?'

'Sure are and you'll see plenty of them on Dartmoor too. Wait till we go to visit my friends Anna and George on the moor. You may even get to ride one of theirs which they have broken in themselves.'

Both Julian and Ruby were avid horse riders and Ruby felt uplifted already after the upsetting experience at Oxford Circus the day before.

'Here we are ... all set Ruby? We get off here.'

Her heart started to race at the thought of meeting Julian's family as if she was about to be put on trial. What will happen if she doesn't measure up?

Chapter Fifteen

'There's Larry waiting on the platform.' The two men hugged then Julian introduced Ruby to his brother.

'Ah, so you're the young lady who has been keeping my young brother on the right track. I'm glad somebody has pulled him into line,' he said, amiably.

'I hear they have forecast freezing weather. I hope it doesn't rain all Christmas,' said Julian, hoping for an enjoyable time with Ruby.

They climbed into Larry's four-wheel drive. Ruby was intrigued with the narrow cobblestone lanes and hedgerows while driving through the countryside outside Cheriton Bishop. She looked hard to see if there were any more wild ponies, but they were nowhere to be seen.

'Hey, Ruby! My wife Maggie has been dying to meet you. She's cooking a special Christmas dinner tomorrow. We're going to have a real traditional English one, just for you.'

Ruby felt they were making far too much fuss of her and appeared embarrassed by all the attention.

After being showered with refreshments and high tea, she asked if she could look around the estate.

'That was exactly what I was thinking. Come on, let's go for a walk,' said Julian, taking her hand and leading her along the narrow path towards the back of the building.

Ruby was blown away by the awesome sight of this magnificent seventeenth-century farmhouse. It had been turned into a lodge in the 1930s. There were originally six stables that were renovated and converted into bedrooms. The building was covered in ivy and the roof a beautiful thatch with shingles at one end.

They even had a gardener who cared for the massive vegetable garden, and everything they used for cooking came straight from the garden including fresh herbs. There were whole paved areas with herbs growing around them. Old fashioned lilac roses ascended the front of the lodge, reaching as far as the roof.

'What do you think Rubes? A far cry from life in Thailand eh? When I grew up, Cheriton Bishop was just a tiny village and life growing up as a boy around here was something I wouldn't have swapped for anything.'

'I think it's not unlike my own village in Cromwell Mead. I would love to have more of a look around the community.'

'I'll check with Maggie to see what time she's expecting us for dinner. We have a chef who is away, but Maggie is a sort of sous-chef and likes to keep on top of things and do things her way.'

'Where shall we go now? What about a walk to that castle you were telling me about that is open to the public?' Ruby remembered there was a castle called Castle Drogo nearby.

'That's not walking distance sorry. I'll ask Larry if I can take the Ford for a spin.'

Ruby saw a castle for the first time in her life. It was in a national historical trust. They spent about half an hour viewing the castle and were about to leave when Julian spotted a colourful poster on a notice board next to the café.

'Look at this Cherry Pie....it's their annual New Year's ball. Looks like it's open to anyone. Would you like to accompany me? I've been wanting to attend one of these for ages and didn't know anyone suitable I could ask. Please, Ruby, it would make me so happy.'

Ruby was taken aback. She had never danced with him before and loved ballroom dancing. She'd received lessons back in Cromwell Mead and had danced a lot as a teen. She too knew nobody suitable as a dance partner.

'Oh. Julian, I'd love that. I can't believe it—a ball at a castle. It sounds unreal!'

***

It was Christmas morning. Ruby was woken by the crowing of a rooster which she hadn't realised had been amongst the free-range hens. She had the best sleep ever in the single, four poster bed with a down filled quilt. She showered and went into the dining room. In the corner of the lounge, she could see a large, exquisitely decorated fir tree with pretty lights. Larry and Maggie had no children and this would have been a sight for sore eyes for little ones. The lodge was usually closed over Christmas but they always had plenty of neighbours drop by with their children.

Julian appeared soon after Ruby, clean-shaven and suave, as usual, dressed in one of his blue silk shirts and new chinos.

'Can we give you a hand Maggie?'

'Not yet. Perhaps when I'm preparing dinner later.

'When are we doing Christmas dinner ... lunch or evening meal?'

'We thought an early meal around four if that suits you both.'

'I'll give you a hand if I can help, Maggie.' Ruby was starting to feel a little redundant. Maggie put her arm around her warmly. 'You're a wee gem, Ruby. I can do with your help later too, thanks.'

After breakfast, Julian and Ruby walked along the river towards the village. It was Sunday and there was a Christmas service at the local church.

'Shall we go to the service, Ruby? I've missed my local church and there are a few people I'd like you to meet.'

Ruby was grateful they both shared the same faith. Their Christian life was very important to them both and they weren't always that free to practice it in Thailand, as they had to be sensitive to the needs of the Islamic and Buddhist residents at Rainbow Haven as well. At least they were able to meet with their little Christian Fellowship group each week in Rayong.

The old stone church was steeped in history. They both enjoyed being back in a traditional church and the message was spot on for Ruby. They stayed for a quick cup of tea, while Julian spotted a few old family friends whom he was very eager to show off his prize to. Ruby felt awkward being bombarded with a lot of personal questions by the old ladies.

'Can we go now? I'm feeling a bit weary if that's okay.' She latched onto Julian's arm, discreetly drawing him away.

As they wandered back to The Gables, the crisp cold air caught Ruby's breath. She was relieved she had carried her woollen coat. Something colder than air touched her cheek, then again. Something glistened on the sleeve of her navy blue coat. A perfectly shaped crystal star.

'Wow! I think it's a snowflake—look!' She yelled out like an excited child. 'I can't believe it, snowing right on Christmas day. What a blessing!'

'Sure is my girl. It happens rarely right on Christmas day though. It must be just for you!' Julian wrapped his arms around her, making sure she was warm enough. 'I have a beanie back at the house for you to wear. You're going to need it from now on.'

The snow started falling rapidly, and fortunately, they both had gloves with them. They frolicked in the snow throwing snowballs at each other like a couple of school children.

'I haven't had this much fun in a long time.' Ruby said, still feeling elated she had seen snow for the first time. 'The snowflakes are so pretty on the branches of those fir trees. It's magical.'

'We'd better be getting back to give Maggie a hand with dinner.' Julian grabbed her hand firmly, leading her back along the riverbank to The Gables.

Christmas dinner with all the trimmings is what Ruby looked forward to after eating mainly Asian food for a year. Though Thai food was very nutritious and appetising, she still missed her traditional foods. Maggie and Larry had gone to a lot of trouble to impress Ruby.

***

The next few days they were busy making plans for the coming weeks. Julian explained to Ruby that before his mother died, he had promised her that he would help Larry keep the lodge going and sort out their business affairs together. He said to Ruby that he'd written to her folks to say he would probably not be able to get back to Thailand until the English spring. He let Ruby know that he would understand if she decided to fly back home. She was in a quandary as to what to do.

***

The New Year's ball came around before they had time to think about it. Maggie wanted to take Ruby out to buy her a ball gown as payment for working hard in the lodge. She'd been up early each morning helping get things ready for the opening of The Gables after New Year.

'Climb in. I know just the shop for you,' Maggie said as she drove the Ford into Exeter. 'It's nice to have your company as I don't have much girl time with The Gables keeping me busy.' Ruby guessed that Maggie must have been about ten years her senior, not old enough to be like a mother but could be the sister she never had.

Together they chose a pile of gowns for Ruby to try on. The one she liked was her favourite colour—a full-length,

104

midnight blue layered dress with silver sequins on the bodice.

'This is it … it's perfect!' she said, not daring to look at the price tag.

'You look like a princess in this, honest you do. Now we just have to get you into a hairdresser, so I must make an appointment for you when we get home.'

Two days later, Ruby was dressed to the nines by Maggie who treated her like a pet poodle. She appeared like a Royal in her midnight blue ball gown with silver shoes covered in sequins, and a clutch bag to match.

Julian looked debonair in his navy blue pinstripe suit with matching waistcoat and shiny black shoes. Ruby fell in love with him all over again.

'You'd better keep an eye on him tonight, Ruby, all dressed to the hilt like that … no, just kidding. I don't think I've ever seen my brother so chic looking. You must have a great effect on him.' Larry elbowed Julian playfully.

Julian screwed up his face at his brother for putting him on the spot in front of Ruby, but it was true. There had never been any reason for him to get dressed like this before.

As they drove to the ball, Julian told Ruby he had spoken to her father on the phone to discuss the staffing at Rainbow Haven and his responsibilities at The Gables. He was concerned, as he knew her parents would not be able to stay for more than a month.

Julian had good news for Ruby. 'Guess what's happening, Rubes. Gamon and Rolando have offered to manage Rainbow Haven with remote support from your folks until I can get back. They are also in a serious relationship which is interesting, so watch the space!'

'That's wonderful, I'm really pleased for Gamon as she is passionate about Rescue Net and so is Rolando … I suppose

Mum and Dad said they need me back at in Cromwell Mead?'

'No … well actually, I hope you don't mind Ruby, but I took the liberty of saying that we could do with some help here if you could stay on with me for two or three months. They didn't mind at all, in fact, they thought the experience would be good for when you get to manage Peace Haven for them one day.'

'Oh, did they now? Mmm.'

'Ruby, if you'd like to give us a hand to establish ourselves and fill in for my mother until we know where we're going with the business, it would be a great help. You'll be on wages so you won't be out of pocket.' It sounded as though Julian was making sure his main investment was safe, which was actually Ruby, and he didn't want to lose her.

'Oh thanks, Julian. I'll discuss it with my parents first over the phone and let you know what I decide. Sounds like a great arrangement.'

Ruby was not the kind of person to be dominated by men and although Julian was not the controlling sort, he was efficient and well organised in business, assertive and confident in any decisions he made.

She wanted to feel free to make her own informed decisions about things too. She had acquired this skill from her mother who had learned the hard way when she'd been married to Ruby's controlling father before he'd died. Cherie had taught her well.

She was also thinking about how good it would be to work alongside Julian at The Gables. He was "sleeping partner" in the business, as he had left his share in the company while Larry and his wife ran the business. Their mother had left the lodge in trust to both her sons.

'I'll give them a call tomorrow and let you know what I decide.'

Julian was slightly perturbed by this, thinking she might decide to go back home to Cromwell Mead on the other side of the world, as she was needed there as well. Peace Haven retreat had gained much popularity over the years and was buoyant as ever. The founders, Belle and Milton were well into their seventies, living in their beach house called Seabird Lodge at Shoal Bay. They visited occasionally to offer their pearls of wisdom and to help out now and then.

Annie and Murray, a semi-retired couple who were also the original staff at Peace Haven, as well as directors, still lived in Lavender Cottage, employed part-time by Cherie and Lyon. But Ruby's parents were also getting on in their mid-fifties and the hospitality work was taxing at times, even though they saw it more as a divine calling, especially the kind of service they gave to the community in Cromwell Mead.

For the rest of the drive to the ball, Ruby and Julian both sat quietly mulling over the conversation they both just had. Were they going to be separated by family responsibilities? Julian began to pray silently—*Please God don't let me lose Ruby now if she is the right one for me. We've been so happy together. I'm sure we could have a good future together.*

'Here we are, Castle Drogo, Guinevere my dear.' He laughed.

'Mmm, parking might be a problem, we should have come earlier.' Within minutes of driving out of the packed carpark, he spotted a space at the side of the building.

Ruby walked tall—the stunning midnight blue gown standing out, gathering attention. As they promenaded into the vast ballroom with the most grandiose sparkling chandeliers Ruby had ever seen, she stopped short in her tracks as she noticed the womens' eyes on her. She could hear whispers—the babble of supposed conjectures about this newcomer to the community. Embarrassed, she hoped they couldn't see the hot flush of her neck, as they couldn't stop gaping at the couple.

Julian jumped in quickly to save her. 'Come over here Rubes,' he said taking her by the hand. 'I want you to meet my friends, family friends I have known since childhood.' The two couples sat at a table ornately decorated with crystal vases filled with deeply fragrant, mini red roses. Ruby began to relax as Andre and Helene made her feel welcome by being non-intrusive in their dialogue with her.

'Another dance, Rubes?'

Julian whisked her off her feet. For an ordinary dancer that he said he was, Ruby hadn't danced with anyone so graceful and light on his feet and easy to follow. She just melted in his arms.

They danced the night away and Ruby couldn't remember when she'd had this much fun dancing. She wanted it to last forever.

What harm would it do if she stayed on until spring? And what then? Eventually, she'd be needed back at Peace Haven so she'd be letting her mother down.

But for now, she is the belle of the ball and she put that on the "back-burner" until another day.

Chapter Seventeen

That night, after the ball, Ruby lay in bed trying to get to sleep in the oversized, four poster bed in one of the guest suites. She always found it a challenge when she was not able to sleep in her own bed at home. What kept going through her mind was the complete paradox between rich and poor she had seen when they met the homeless people in London near Harrods in Knightsbridge.

Why is there so much inequality in the world? She asked herself. And those snooty women at the ball in their over-dressed hats and affected speech. Not Julian's friends, they are genuine— but many of the other people are so shallow and materialistic.

She continued to remonstrate with herself as though trying to come to some sort of conclusion or decision after she had heard a nearby woman talking about her latest property deal and her new Alpha Romeo.

She kept thinking about the magical evening she had just spent with Julian which uplifted her. How lovely of him to invite her to partner him at the ball. He had been so attentive and romantic, the perfect gentleman. It was a night to remember.

As she drifted off to sleep, she began to imagine what life would be like with Julian in it permanently. Where would they live? England, Thailand, or New Zealand? She drifted into oblivion.

***

The Gables was in full swing after New Year's Day. Ruby fitted in well and Maggie had her organised from daylight to dark, but in a pleasant way and Ruby was glad of the work experience in the five-star hotel.

Ruby began to feel uneasy about where all this was heading. She asked herself how Julian could really expect her to up and leave her family behind to settle in England. He kept on telling her that it would all fall into place if it was meant to be and whatever they both decided, it would be for the best. She knew she had to trust God no matter what, as he had never let her down.

***

Spring arrived in Devon, one of the most picturesque places to be at this time of the year. The country lanes were lined with wildflowers and the moors came to life with an abundance of wildlife and purple or pink Heather.

It was Julian and Ruby's day off. They job-shared with Larry and Maggie so they were able to arrange their days off together. Julian's mother had played a big part in the business, knew the ropes well, and the adjustment without her to manage the hotel was a challenge for Larry and Maggie. They were grateful for the help Julian and Ruby gave them temporarily.

'Cook has packed us a picnic basket, Ruby, so all you need is a sunhat and some good walking shoes,' said Julian.

He stood waiting for her by the rose garden. She stepped onto the veranda dressed in a white cotton dress Maggie had given her and a pair of blue Plimsolls. Her wavy, flaxen sun-bleached hair, billowing in the fresh breeze, made her appear like a movie star on a film set. Julian had to catch himself and get his feet back on the ground.

'I want to take you somewhere special. It's a blessing this mild weather. It's not usually as warm at this time of the year. Buckle up!'

As the car hurtled down the driveway onto the lane, Julian suddenly slowed down, remembering how hazardous the country lanes are and that he had a precious cargo onboard.

Ruby soaked up the ambience of the beautiful English countryside which made her feel relaxed. It was the place where she thrived best.

'Look out the window to your left, quickly!' Julian pointed towards a family of brown hares chasing each other near the hedgerow. Bright yellow daffodils lined the road and now and then she spotted clumps of snowdrops under the trees.

They headed up onto Dartmoor. The windy road to Anna and George's sheep farm seemed to take forever and Ruby wondered how anyone could live in such an isolated spot.

'Hey, stop for a minute—look over there!' Ruby bellowed. She pointed in the direction of a herd of ponies grazing on the side of the road.

'Please, Julian let's stop here for our picnic. There are a lot more over there, look!'

Ruby was ecstatic. She'd never seen wild horses before. There were all kinds of ponies in different colours and sizes. One of them reminded her of a childhood pony she had called Pinto which had brown and white patches. Her parents had to sell him in the end as he bucked her off a few times and wasn't to be trusted. She had five horses in succession, the last being her sweetheart, a cream show pony called Vicky which had the sweetest nature.

'Oh okay, just be careful not to startle them. Remember they are wild and if vexed they can bite and kick. We can take that path over there.' Julian had spotted a walkway along the side of a river.'

As they wandered towards the riverbank, they noticed that the river was swollen in parts due to the melting snow on the hills.

'Look at that, a new-born foal, probably only days old ... how amazing.' Ruby's eyes widened like saucers as she took out her camera.

'Don't get too close Rubes, that mare will be over-protective right now.'

Julian appeared more over-protective of Ruby than the mare was toward her foal which Ruby ignored.

The ponies appeared to be quite used to people, as the moor was full of families having picnics right through the summer months.

Ruby spread the rug out on a dry grassy patch under a large oak tree. Julian looked inside the hamper that Cook had packed. 'I used to do this as a child when our cook would often put little treats inside for me.'

'Anything interesting this time?' Ruby sat hovering over the basket.

'Mmm— smoked salmon from our own pool and chicken drumsticks. She's made fresh raspberry tarts and home-made lemonade.'

Ruby's favourites were the sweet ripe cherries from their orchard.

As they sat finishing their lunch, there was a rustling sound from behind. Ruby almost jumped out of her skin. Staring right at them was a frisky young filly, probably a yearling. It was coal black, with a white nose, and just stood there watching them.

'Perhaps they're used to people feeding them', she whispered.

'Here, roll this apple over towards her to see if she takes it,' Julian whispered.

Ruby took the apple and very gently rolled it towards the filly, then kept very still. Almost ravenously, she gobbled it up with great speed and cautiously took a few steps closer.

'Julian, quick, take my camera out of my bag and capture this if you can.'

'It's okay I have mine in my pocket.'

He took a series of photos, also trying to get Ruby in the foreground. When he had finished, he took her arm and pulled her towards him.

'Ruby, I need to talk to you about something.'

'What is it, what's wrong?'

'Nothing wrong, but something has come up that I need to sort out and I have to go to London for a day. It's better that I go alone as I need to see my mother's lawyer, something to do with the estate.'

'That's okay, I'm sure I'll be busy here. Maggie has organised me quite well so I won't be at a loose end.'

'I mean tomorrow … it's your day off too. I'll probably stay overnight with Mrs D as I arranged to dine with an old colleague I haven't caught up with in years.'

'Oh, I see. Perhaps I could take myself off and do some orienteering for the day.'

'The other thing I wanted to tell you … I had a letter from your father. He and your mother are back in Cromwell Mead.'

'I know already, Mum wrote to me too.' She pressed a finger against her lips. 'Shish, wait … something startled the ponies and they took off.' A couple of foxes rushed past, chasing the ponies, but Ruby knew they were no match for the wild ponies, and relaxed again back into Julian's arms.

'Your father has left Gamon and Rolando in charge of Rainbow Haven until I can get back. He has also asked if I'm happy to continue as a coordinator or whether I would like to hand it over to Gamon and Rolando completely. Apparently, they are in a serious relationship. It means I'll have to go over there soon and meet with them all to discuss my intentions.'

Ruby was disappointed at having to leave the rolling hills of Devon, though she didn't enjoy the winter and disliked the cold. She knew that summer in Devon didn't last long and she didn't look forward to another winter in England.

Julian started packing up their picnic basket and stood up. 'We'll have to get going now if we want to get to see Anna and George and ride the horses on the moor.'

They folded up the blanket, grabbed the hamper, and sped towards the car.

As the vehicle meandered its way up the windy road towards Kestor, they could see smoke in the air from the cottage chimney, and as they drove closer, they saw snow lying on the ridge. The farm was high up and the snow hadn't melted there yet.

***

Chapter Eighteen

George and Anna's cottage was made from stone off the moor. It had a low roof and was primitive in appearance. Their property was so remote and barren that not many people could cope with living such an austere lifestyle.

As they approached the cottage, Anna waved to them from the doorstep. She appeared eager to see them, probably due to her social isolation, as she was a gregarious woman while her husband George who was more reserved.

'It's so good to see you, Julian. Let me take a look at Ruby.'

She stood in front of Ruby, looking her over like a farmer inspecting a new workhorse. Ruby felt uncomfortable but quickly observed that she was a warm, hospitable and motherly sort. Neither Anna nor George had Devonshire accents. They had both been educated at private schools and were university graduates.

'You're just like I imagined. I have so looked forward to meeting you. I've lunch ready and then I want to take you for a ride over the moor.'

'Anna! Have they arrived already?' George called from the back of the house. He hastened to meet Ruby. 'I'm so pleased to meet you and Julian has told us so much about you, only good things, mind.' He winked at Julian and took their coats.

'Come on you lot, the food's ready. Get it while it's warm,' said Anna.

They wandered into the dining room where Julian remembered he had to duck his head so he wouldn't hit the ceiling. The inside of the house was constructed from plaster and stone, with heavy wooden rafters. Ruby loved the big stone fireplace, and the fire was roaring when they walked in.

'I hope you're going to like my farmhouse soup. It's my grandmother's recipe and has been in the family for years. I baked some wholemeal bread to go with it.' Anna was proud of her culinary skills.

'Ruby, have you ever seen a hydro-electric power supply? We've made a little dam on the farm which supplies all our power. I'll take you both down after lunch to see it. The snow's starting to melt so there's plenty of water to run it,' said George, competing with his wife for their attention.

'Ah, not until we've been for a ride on the moor, George. I've already booked her.' Anna laughed and gathered up the soup plates. 'I hope you've room for dessert,' she called out from the tiny kitchen that looked like a ship's galley.

'You've gone to too much trouble.' Ruby looked bug-eyed as Anna placed the dessert on the table with a pot of clotted cream.

'I hope you like apple pie. The fruit is grown here, our best-kept secret. So is our homemade cider.' George carried in a large jug of cider and placed it on the table. 'Drink both of you?'

'Just a small one for me thanks.' Ruby remembered that Devon cider is potent and last time went straight to her head.

'Just the one thanks. I am driving.' Julian followed suit.

Ruby felt spoilt, as she hadn't tasted apple pie since she had left Peace Haven where the women there often made apple or berry pie. 'Mmm, do you mind if I take a little more? This is delicious.'

'Not at all. As long as poor Sally, the mare you'll be riding can carry you.'

They rested for a bit after lunch and then George took Julian to look around the farm.

'Here, Ruby ... I think these Jodhpur trousers will fit you and you'll need to wear a helmet ... try this one for size.'

Ruby slipped into the bathroom to try on the trousers. 'They fit okay thanks.'

'Here, take this too. It'll be cold up on the hills. This Swanndri will stop that cutting wind on the Tor.'

Ruby's horse Sally, a tall bay mare was docile and friendly, which made up for its intimidating height.

Anna went on ahead of her then stopped on the ridge. Ruby, wary of the thick snow on the ground, was afraid there might be rabbit holes hiding under the snow. She had never ridden in such conditions before.

Anna and George, a middle-aged couple lived a rugged lifestyle. Ruby wished she could be as resilient Anna who appeared a proper English lady but strong and self-reliant. Ruby was impressed that they were almost self-sufficient in that they grew all their own vegetables and they ate beef, lamb, and chicken which their own animals provided. They had the meat prepared by a butcher in

'Isn't this an amazing view, Ruby? Look out there. You can see right across Dartmoor.' Anna pulled her black gelding alongside her. 'See down there.' She pointed to the back of the farm where George had taken Julian. 'That's where the hydro-electric system is next to that river.'

'Wow, that's amazing generating your own power. What else do you do that's self-sustaining?' Ruby really did have an interest, as her own parents were right into self-sufficiency at Peace Haven, though not to this extent.

'We use milk from the house cow. That's where the clotted cream came from. Except of course I had to clot it.' Anna appeared amused. 'We get fresh free range eggs each day and we have our own orchard. Yes, mostly self-sufficient.'

The horses, though sure-footed, took their time descending the steep hill through the soft snow down to the back of the farm. The men had left the dam and dark clouds were appearing overhead. Ruby was over-awed with seeing the great achievement in generating their own electricity from scratch. This was an education in itself.

'We'd better get these horses back into their stalls, Ruby. They'll need a rub down and blankets put on for the night.'

Julian came to the stables to meet them. 'I'm sorry, Anna, but I will have to steal Ruby away from you now. I think the roads will be dicey driving back with all this sleet, and it's getting dark.'

Ruby felt stiff from not having ridden for a few years. She was pleased to have been rescued.

As they drove back home around the windy, wet roads they swapped notes.

'They are an amazing couple. I've never seen a farm that self-sufficient before.'

'They were really taken with you Rubes and asked me to bring you back again soon.'

'That may not happen if you end up going back to Thailand, now will it.' Ruby sounded slightly vexed, not knowing where she was going to end up with all the changes. Julian went quiet during the rest of the trip back to The Gables.

They arrived at The Gables just in time to meet the postman at the gate. Julian took the mail from him and started sifting through the pile.

'Here, Rubes. One for you it seems—it has an Australian stamp on it.' He handed her an envelope that was postmarked Bonalbo.

'Oh, thanks. At last a letter from Kate. I'm dying to catch up on her news.'

He left her in peace to read the letter from her friend and wandered inside the house. Ruby sat on the garden seat nodding her head and smiling as she read Kate's news—that she'd already enrolled in a twelve-month distance study course for veterinary nursing and was now an official employee in Merv's veterinary clinic. It appeared to be a whirlwind romance and Kate had written to her parents and told them she was there to stay. But Ruby wondered how long Kate would be able to withstand the extreme isolation of this quaint rural community. Time would tell, she decided.

***

The next day, the train to London was half empty this time as it chugged into Exeter station. Ruby had felt butterflies in her stomach at being separated from Julian, even though it was just for a day or two.

'Cheer up, Pie, I'll be back before you know it. I'll bring you something ... a surprise.'

'I'm fine, honest. I have plenty to do. Go well and I'll see you back here soon.' She kissed him gently on the cheek, momentarily leaning her head on his chest then waved and walked off.

Ruby drove back to The Gables trying to decide what to do on her days off for the next two days. She felt like having an adventure, as she'd not had one for quite some time.

'Why don't you take yourself off and do some sightseeing, Ruby?' Maggie folded the clothes she had just taken off the clothesline.

'It's strange, as up until now, Julian and I have always spent our days off together. Maybe it'll be good for me to have some alone time.'

Ruby knew she would never really be alone as she always felt God's presence wherever she went. That's why she wasn't afraid of anything.

'Why don't you take a trip down to Cornwall to see your friend? You'll love it down there. You could always book into the backpackers in Penzance. If she isn't there you could just have a good look around. We won't mind you taking the Ford if you want or there is a train that goes from Cheriton Cross that takes about two hours to get to Penzance. I can drop you at the station after lunch if you don't want to drive.'

***

Ruby preferred the train as she could see the scenery rather than concentrate on driving on unfamiliar roads. The train ride to Cornwall was spectacular. She sat next to a friendly old Australian couple on the train who chatted to her all about her work with Rescue Net and about their own lives back in New South Wales. She asked them if they knew her friends in Bonalbo, New South Wales.

They laughed. 'Do you know how big New South Wales is? It's over eight hundred thousand square kilometres, compared to approximately fifteen hundred square kilometres in London.'

Ruby's face went crimson with embarrassment and she quickly excused her ignorance.

'Don't worry sweetie, Charlie only knows that because he's a retired history and geography teacher.'

Ruby was quiet for the rest of the trip. As she sat looking at the view, she saw landscape similar to that of her hometown Cromwell Mead. Lush and green with multiple farmlets scattered about. She felt a touch of homesickness for the first time. It hadn't been an issue up until now as she'd always had Julian to distract her.

At the backpackers, Ruby was commandeered by a chatty elderly couple soon after she had booked in. They asked her to join them for lunch. It seemed to her that old people were always wanting to take her under their wings.

They introduced themselves. 'Hubert and Olive MacKenzie. Come and join us.'

They opened a basket of food and pulled out a packet of strange looking objects that looked like dumplings.

'Have you ever seen these delicacies before Ruby? Do you know what they are?'

Ruby detected a strong Scottish accent. She looked at the small squishy-looking brown balls of what looked like sausage skins with meat inside.

'They look like sheep testicles or something! Yuk.'

'They both laughed. That's what everyone says,' the woman replied. 'No, they aren't. They're made from a mixture of sheep's organs, oats, and spices. A Scottish delicacy called Haggis—try some.'

Ruby tried hard to be polite and taste the strange looking food. 'Mmm, that's tasty, really nice. Thank you.'

The doting couple showed her the directions into Penzance. She loved the sense of freedom, feeling the sea breeze in her hair while watching the fishing boats coming and going. She bought an ice-cream from the street-side vendor and wandered into the harbour to look for her friend's house following a map the receptionist at the backpackers gave her. She had tried to find her phone number in the local directory to no avail but she had her home address. She found the house, a small plaster cottage, white-washed with rambling pink roses out front. Ruby looked through the front windows. It looked quiet. She went to knock on the door when she heard a woman's voice from behind, 'Excuse me ... are you looking for Mandy and Pete? They have gone to London for a holiday. They obviously weren't expecting you.'

Ruby felt disappointed but knew she was taking a chance just turning up like that.

'Would you mind giving Mandy a letter if I write a quick note for her?'

'Not at all, I can give you some writing paper if you like.'

'I'd appreciate that. I feel pretty stupid, as I should have written to ask if she was going to be home if I visited.'

'Don't worry. Why don't you come in for a nice cup of tea before you go?' Ruby welcomed the offer, as she was feeling a bit peckish.

'Here we are dear. I made some fresh scones this morning. Would you like one with a bit of raspberry jam? How do you like your tea?'

Ruby sat looking around the tiny cottage. It was very quaint, almost like a doll's house. They all appeared to live a simple life in this village by the sea. The people in Cornwall seemed so much like the community in her own hometown in Cromwell Mead. She tried to shrug off her feeling of homesickness. Even though she'd set out on an adventure to experience a bit of freedom, she did enjoy the company of this stranger who waved goodbye as she walked on down the street to find the way back to the backpackers.

She woke in the morning to a radiant, bright sunny day with a clear blue sky and the sound of seagulls overhead. She had a perfect sea view from her bedroom window where she could see the fishing boats arriving back from a night's fishing. She could smell breakfast cooking, something nostalgic wafting through her bedroom door. She dressed and went along the hallway into the kitchen. The Scottish couple were there, bright and chirpy, cooking bacon and eggs.

'Are you hungry lass? We've plenty of tucker here if you'd like some.'

'Oh, no thanks, I just need a coffee first thing, then I'll have some of the muesli I brought with me. But that's very kind of you thank you.'

'What are you going to do today, young lady?' Hubert asked.

'I have to get back today as I could only stay for one night. I need to return to Cheriton Bishop.'

'Well, well, I would never have guessed. You aren't from around here, are you? I don't detect a West Country accent at all. Are you visiting people in Cheriton Bishop?'

'Yes, my friend Julian's family. I'm from New Zealand and have been working in Thailand as an aid worker for trafficked victims.'

'That's a wonderful thing to do, the poor beggars. I'll bet you have seen some pretty dark things happening over there. Is it a religious organisation you were with?'

'No, not really, but some of us on the staff, including the founders, are from a Christian background, although the organisation caters for everyone.'

'How are you going to get back to Cheriton Bishop? We can take you to the other side of Bovey Tracey and drop you at the bus stop. Cheriton Bishop is not that far from there. It'll be much cheaper than taking the train all the way there,' said Olive, treating her like a grandchild.

'Thanks, I would appreciate that. I just need to finish packing and drop off my room key at reception. I'll be ready in about ten minutes if that's okay.'

Olive and her husband continued to be very chatty the whole way to Bovey Tracey. Ruby heard about their whole family history, the clan Mackenzie. History was Ruby's worst subject at school, and above all, she really disliked genealogy and found it boring. She was nearly asleep, lulled by the incessant chatter of Olive's voice in the front seat.

Chapter Nineteen

'Here we are! Just pull over there Hubert— there's the bus shelter,' she said, directing Hubert officiously.

While Hubert was taking her rucksack out of the boot of the car, Olive grabbed Ruby's hand and popped something into it. 'Shush— this is a little something towards your holiday. You have given to others generously in your aid work and it doesn't hurt to receive sometimes, either.'

Ruby was shocked as Olive placed a fifty-pound note in her hand.

'Bless you Olive, bless you heaps! I don't know what to say.'

'You just keep up the good work. The Lord knows and he rewards you in other ways when you least expect it.'

Ruby took their address so she could send them a postcard from home someday. For now, she must get on the next bus that comes. Fortunately, she had her bus timetable with her and could see if she was on the right bus route. She waited for nearly two hours with no sign of a bus.

She couldn't understand what was going on with the buses, as Olive assured her they came every hour. Then suddenly she remembered – 'Today is a Public Holiday! Oh no, what am I going to do,' she uttered in despair, as she didn't like not feeling in control.

She was about a mile out of the village and the road was empty, not a vehicle in sight as the weather changed and clouded over so that dusk started to descend very quickly. She began to walk out of town in the wrong direction, unbeknown to her and came to a crossroads. She took out her torch and pointed it at the signpost that read KESTOR

INN. She remembered seeing this sign when she visited Anna and George.

She thought if she headed towards Kestor, she would meet either a bus or a local person who would give her a ride to Cheriton Cross. She began to feel vulnerable. Suddenly the fog thickened with each step she took and became like pea soup so that she could see nothing, not even a metre in front of her. She felt afraid, even panicky and remembered Julian had told her that Dartmoor prison was on the moor and several murders had taken place there over the years. Some of them were serial murders and occasionally prisoners were known to escape onto the moor. She hoped he just told her that to tease her, but then she remembered seeing something on the news about it several years ago. She also knew that the area was full of bogs that could swallow a person up, which was a huge deterrent for escaping prisoners.

She felt like an idiot and should have taken the train from Penzance. The Scottish couple were so insistent, what could she do? Ruby pulled herself up for berating herself, as this was not her fault. It was just unfortunate that the buses didn't happen to be running on this particular day, just unfortunate!

She thought she heard a sound behind her, a strange scuffling sound that sent a chill down her spine. It seemed to stop momentarily then she heard it again. This time it seemed to be closer. Her heart started racing. She remembered there was a small camping penknife in the side pocket of her rucksack and grabbed it out quickly, feeling sick inside with fear. 'Please God, take away my fear... protect me!'

She tried hard to refrain from bursting into tears, as she needed her wits about her now. She started to pray in desperation—'*Please Lord, I don't know what to do, I'm afraid, and you said that you may not always remove the storm but you would give us peace through the storm. Please God, take away my fear so that I can think clearly. Please direct my path.'*

Ruby opened her eyes as she heard a rustling in the bushes next to her. She couldn't swallow the lump in her throat. As she directed her torchlight towards the hedge, there stood an inquisitive red fox staring at her, whimpering as if it was talking to her. It appeared almost tame. She cried with relief.

'Hello— what are you doing out here?' She was glad of the company and it just stood there watching her then ran off.

She wondered if a bus would still come, or perhaps one of the locals might come by and give her a ride to Anna and George's farm. *What if it's still miles away?*

Just as she began to feel weary from all the walking, she saw in the distance what vaguely looked like a farm cottage with lights on. Thank You, God!

She believed by faith that it was going to be safe for her to approach the house, as she believed in divine intervention. As she stumbled forward towards the front of the house, she caught sight of a billboard. Again she used her torchlight to read what it said—

FRESH FREE RANGE EGGS

FREE RANGE CHICKENS

She was sure she'd seen that sign recently ... 'I know,' she uttered. 'On the way to Anna and George's house. Perhaps these people know them, as this house is not that far away.'

She knocked warily on the heavy, wooden oak door. Someone stirred inside. She kept her hand on the penknife in her pocket. A light went on and the door opened. There stood a stooped old woman, face weathered by the harsh Dartmoor climate. She had bravely dared to open the door to a stranger on such a night. Perhaps an angel in disguise, Ruby thought.

'Well, well, what have we here?' The woman stood staring at the rucksack and the weary look on Ruby's face was obvious. 'Come closer, me darling— what brings thee here?'

'I'm so sorry, I'm lost ... lost in the fog and the bus never turned up.'

'Where thee be going?' She spoke with such a strong Devonshire accent that Ruby could barely follow her, especially some of her dialect.

'I'm trying to get home to Cheriton Bishop but took the wrong road at the crossroads. I have friends at Kestor, near the Inn and thought you might know them. Anna and George ... I don't know them by their last name, sorry.'

'Not me dear, I don't. I kinda keep to myself nowadays. My phone's not working either due to that darn storm we had here. Come and get yourself dry by mee fire. I've just stoked it up a heap.'

Ruby was grateful to be able to sit down for a while, especially in a warm place. She felt as though the thick fog had penetrated her soul. She sensed intuitively, that this woman could help her get home to Julian.

'You eat this mee dear— you look like you haven't had a decent feed today. I got some rabbit stew with herbs and my own apple scrumpy that'll give thee a good boost.'

Ruby felt sleepy after the home-made apple cider but knew she had to get back. Julian would be worried sick as she had been due back today and there was no way of contacting him. If the woman could give her a lift to Anna and George's she could phone him from there.

'Thanks so much for the lovely food and your kind hospitality, Meg. I hope you don't mind me asking, but I was wondering if you could please drop me up to our friends, not far from you in Kestor.'

'Aww, so sorry mee luv, I don't drive. But don't ye worry, I can sort it for you, sweetie. Tomorrow morning my son Edward is arriving for a visit around ten. He's in the Naval Base in Plymouth and has a few days off. I'll ask him to take thee to Cheriton Bishop ... how's that?'

'Oh, that's very kind of you ... sure he won't mind?'

'Not at all. He be a generous sort, in fact, I think he been to The Gables a few times. He be an officer and they've had a few functions and banquets there. The owners will know him.'

Ruby was relieved to know that, as she wasn't so sure about travelling to Cheriton Bishop with a strange man. He could be a psychopath, for all she knows. In spite of this, she started to see that God really was taking care of her.

***

Back at The Gables, Julian was indeed worried sick but he too had prayed for help that Ruby would be safe.

'I'll bet you she's had so much fun at the backpackers that she ran out of time and decided to stay on another night,' Maggie reassured him.

'But I know Ruby well. She'd be thinking of others and not want people to be worried about her. She would have phoned me.'

'What if she didn't write down our phone number, which is highly likely?' Larry could see the look of trepidation on Julian's face.

'I've already phoned the backpackers. They said she left before midday with an elderly Scottish couple who were giving her a ride part of the way. I think I'll get the car and go and look for her.' Julian looked pale, Larry noticed. 'Look, mate, you can't go out there now... it's heavy fog and you can't see anything. Wait till the morning and I'll help you look.'

'No, Larry if she hasn't turned up or made contact by the morning, I'll go to the local police and file a missing person report.'

Julian took himself off to his room, trying to stifle the sick feeling in the pit of his stomach. He kept berating himself for going off to go to London. 'That's ridiculous', he said to himself, of course, I have to be able to separate myself from my girlfriend for a day, even a week or longer without worrying something bad will happen. Stop playing God and let up on yourself!'

He realised he hadn't asked God's help and when things were going well, going his way, he found it a challenge to let go and let God. He had always thought he could work things out himself. This time he was stumped— powerless, helpless *'Sorry, God I've been taking things into my own hands so much lately. I can't really work everything out myself, and this time, I have no answers. Please don't let anything bad happen to Ruby... I love her, even though I haven't said anything to her yet. Show me what to do. I ask you for peace of mind and your guidance. Thank you.'*

Chapter Twenty

'Ruby, come eer me girl and have some breakfast before you leave eer. I can't have ye going off with an empty tummy now can I?' Meg brought out some scrambled eggs cooked on her wood range oven. Ruby observed how orange the eggs were compared to the pale looking things in the grocery store. She was still struggling to understand the woman's unusual broken English.

'Ah, free range eggs! Mmm, they look good. Thanks so much, Meg.'

'Have some more toast,' said Meg, handing her another piece of her whole grain toast in one hand and a jar of marmalade in the other.

'I did bake that there bread this morning while you were still asleep.'

'Thanks, heaps! Meg—how long have you lived here? Have you always lived here on your own?' Ruby had noticed the size of the property.

'I been a widow several years. Been a struggle at times, but my boy— he comes to give me a hand on weekly leave. I hope I'll end me days on this farm. They can carry me out in a box!'

Ruby noticed Meg didn't spend much time on her personal grooming. Her ragged dress was worn—her long, bedraggled, grey hair made her appear like a witch, and she had front teeth missing.

There were hens running everywhere, even in the house, and a milking cow in the barn. In another barn, she saw a small herd of white goats with their kids.

'Aw, they are so cute. What do you use them for— milk?'

'They are Angora goats, Ruby. I send their wool off to the markets and use some of the milk for me own use.'

There was a knock at the door. Meg hurried to open it.

'Edward, I'm so glad you're here early. Come and meet Ruby.'

A tall handsome man entered in his navy uniform, quite different to what Ruby imagined he would be like. He appeared well educated, unlike his mother whose English language was poor along with her strong West Country accent. He sat down with a cup of tea after Meg brushed off one of her armchairs.

'Have thee eaten, son?' His mother had left some food for him on the range.'

'I have thanks. I was up early as I had some business to do in Plymouth.'

Ruby was watching him, trying to work out how old he would be. She guessed in his early forties. I hope he doesn't get ideas if he takes me to The Gables.

'Well, what have we got planned today? What brings you here Ruby?'

Meg jumped in and explained to Edward how Ruby lost her way in the fog. 'You remember those folk who run The Gables in Cheriton Bishop?'

'Oh yes, we've used their restaurant for officers' functions for several years. Ah, Larry and ...'

'Maggie,' replied Ruby. 'Larry is my friend Julian's brother. Julian is a colleague of mine from the aid organisation I am involved with in Thailand and we have been dating. He brought me here to meet his family.'

'Mmm, that sounds serious?' He smiled and winked at her. 'I can drive you back there if you like. I need to help Mum around the farm for a few hours first.'

'Ah, good, I have a pile of logs that need splitting for firewood.' Meg rubbed her hands together with delight and went out to oversee her son chopping wood while Ruby wandered out to see the baby goats. Meg walked over to join her. 'Ruby, I have just the thing for thee, something special thee could do before leaving eer.'

'What's that Meg?

'I can show thee how to bottle feed the baby goats for me. I'll just go heat their milk.' Ruby followed her inside. 'And what does thee think of me fine boy, he's a looker isn't he?'

Ruby felt embarrassed and didn't know what to say.

'Is he single? It would be hard for a man to have a wife in the Navy I would think.'

'Uh-uh, my precious boy bats for the other side ... he likes the fellas. I've never seen him with a lady. But he do be an ardworkin fella, my Edward.'

'What a waste! Do you have other children?'

'For sure, I have a daughter who lives in London. She's a real goody that one. She be engaged to be wed soon.'

'Mum, where do you want me to stack this wood?' Edward walked in just as the conversation finished.

Whew, that was close, thought Ruby. It would have been awful if he had heard his mother talking about him like that.

Meg handed Edward some of her fresh baked bread to take back to the naval base with him. Her face showed a twinge of sadness as he set off. Ruby was in the passenger seat.

'What do you think of my mother, Ruby—a hard case isn't she? I think she's quite lonely really, but she won't move from there. I wanted her to move to Plymouth. It was probably hard for you to grasp her broken English but I'm used to it.'

Ruby just smiled and preferred not to comment.

As they drove out onto the main road towards Moreton Hampstead, Ruby thought she should try to phone Julian.

'I need to find a phone as my friends will be worried sick about me. I haven't been able to reach them for the past twenty-four hours.'

'That's no problem. There is a phone box near here. I'll stop for you. Do you have any coins?'

'Yes, I do thanks.'

About a mile along the road, he pulled over next to a red phone box.

Maggie answered and nearly went hysterical as she called out to Julian to come to the phone.

'Is that you, Ruby? Where are you for goodness sake? I have just been talking to the police. What's happened, I've been worried sick?' Julian's voice stammered.

'I'm about twenty minutes away. Someone is bringing me home. I'm okay now but I got lost on the moor. I'll tell you about it when I see you.'

Chapter Twenty-one

Ruby almost felt guilty of putting Julian and his family through all the stress. But it was not her fault. She had trusted that the Scottish couple knew what they were talking about when they said she could get a bus from Bovey Tracey. It was just human error. She forgave herself and them for their oversight.

Edward drove along the windy lanes slowly, as though he wasn't used to carrying passengers. 'Your family must have been beside themselves with worry, I expect. Good thing you found my mother's place before the night set in. There are some weirdos around Dartmoor occasionally. There's a mental asylum near Bovey Tracey and sometimes they get out.'

Ruby was relieved she hadn't been told this before she got lost on the moor.

As the car drew near the front gate of The Gables, Ruby could see the outline of Julian standing waiting for her to arrive. He appeared anxious. As Edward's Audi cruised slowly towards him, Julian rushed up to the vehicle, barely waiting for it to pull up before he tried to open Ruby's passenger door.

'Ruby, thank God you're alright. I've been beside myself. Hi there ... who have we here Ruby?'

As Ruby approached Julian to greet him with a kiss, he frowned and turned his head away for the first time.

'Julian, this is Edward ... his mother kindly rescued me off the moor when I lost my way and he offered to bring me back here.' He voice shook. She was almost in tears and couldn't bear thinking that she may have caused Julian to mistrust her in any way.

'Thanks so much for looking after her. We expected her back yesterday and imagined all kinds of things when she didn't turn up last night.'

'Will you come inside for a cup of tea, perhaps, Edward?' Ruby wanted to show her gratitude but looked sideways at Julian.

'No, I can't this time sorry, I have to drive to Exeter then get back to the base. Perhaps another time.'

The two of them waved Edward off and Julian hastily escorted Ruby back inside to hear the whole story with Larry and Maggie in tow. When she'd finished, they were all so relieved no harm had come to her, especially Julian.

'Rubes, we were particularly worried as a dangerous psychiatric patient has escaped from the mental hospital onto the moor and hasn't been found yet. He could have been near you, for all we know. That's what worried me the most.'

'Well, I'm sure glad I didn't hear that news before I arrived at the bus stop in Bovey Tracey. It was bad enough without that to frighten me.'

'Oh, poor Ruby, I really thought I had lost you, I couldn't help but fear the worst. Young girls often get accosted on the moor when they go off alone.'

Ruby felt sorry for Julian and felt bad that he had been distraught.

The next morning, he took Ruby to a local café for breakfast so they could talk and make plans.

'I've been to see my lawyer and signed a few papers. The Gables is in a trust for Larry and me, and I've left my share in it until Larry and Maggie get themselves sorted. They are only going to run it as a Bed and Breakfast after I've gone as it has become too much to provide full meals and accommodation now that my mother has gone.' Ruby felt honoured that Julian trusted her enough to discuss his financial affairs with her.

'I thought that Cook does all the meals.'

'He does the cooking, but it's all the day to day planning and buying in supplies that takes work. Then there's the laundry, that's huge. There's just the two of them now and it's hard going.'

'You wouldn't stay on permanently to help them as part of the business then?'

'It's not how I want to spend my future. It was a lifestyle choice for my parents for years which Larry and Maggie are keen on. I prefer to use my qualifications in helping the "underdog" or those who are marginalised, and the poor.'

Ruby admired his humanity and his values which were close to her heart.

'That's why I took the role on at Rescue Net.' Ruby said proudly. 'What have you decided to do then?'

'I'll have to go back to Rainbow Haven and make sure everything is running the way it should be and that we have sufficient staffing levels.'

'Okay ... I could come with you too.'

'I was hoping you would say that Rubes, as I thought you may have decided to go back home to your parents.'

'No way, I'm not going to let you go that easily.' She watched the reaction on his face for more evidence of his true feelings for her.

Julian stepped towards her, taking her in his arms. He cupped her face in his strong hands, looked her in the eye. 'Ruby, I love you, don't you see that? I've loved you right from the outset when we spent the day at the botanical gardens together in Thailand. I was just holding back, as I didn't know if the feelings were mutual.'

Ruby decided not to hold back anymore either. Her lips found his and she kissed him passionately so that he would know for sure what her words could not express.

'I couldn't stop thinking about you after you left Rayong to go to Devon. I felt I was going to lose you then, especially when you didn't reply to my letter. I was so confused.'

'I'm really sorry, Ruby, but I was torn, in a kind of dilemma at that stage, and pretty much in shock that my mother had gone for good. What with the funeral and having to help Larry keep the business going, I didn't want to make any commitments then.'

'Well, we're together now, that's all that matters.' Ruby breathed a sigh of relief, as she no longer felt bewildered.

'Where do we go from here? I've told Larry that I'll have to get back to my job in Rayong, so that's no problem.'

'Let's go ahead and book some tickets then.'

***

Ruby was sad to leave scenic Devon behind, especially when the landscape reminded her so much of her home in Cromwell Mead. The green rolling hills, wild ponies, and the unique English wildlife are special, but she must remember what her primary purpose in life is— not to seek endless self-gratification, but to help those her are suffering and worse off than herself.

This is what she kept telling herself, but was she convinced?

Julian didn't feel that sadness. Instead, he was elated that he could, at last, get back to his main vocation in life to seek and save the lost, in human terms.

'The next train is ours, Ruby, so we'd better get to platform four.' Julian startled her as she sat watching a radiant blue kingfisher sitting on an overhead powerline.

'Larry will be sorry to see you go … still … you've been here a long time and given him a lot of support. You have to leave sooner or later.'

'He is very capable, so is Maggie, and they'll do well. They both have a good head for business.'

Ruby thought about her parents running their retreat back home at Peace Haven— hard work at their time in life in their late fifties. But the founders of Peace Haven, Belle and Milton were into their seventies when they gave up, she assured herself. Ruby was trying to justify not having to rush back home to help them. But she was an adult and had her own life to lead and was not beholden to her parents. They could manage quite well without her. Deep down, her loyalty was divided, even though she wasn't married to Julian.

Ruby sat back on the train, once again soaking up the picturesque Devon landscape— undulating green fields and quaint farmlets as the train chugged past. She had grown to love the ambience of this countryside and was reluctant to leave it all behind her. If Julian had decided to stay and run The Gables with Larry and Maggie, she wouldn't have minded.

***

Julian picked up a local newspaper and tried to concentrate on reading it, but his mind couldn't focus. He was more concerned with what Ruby was thinking. Is she going to stay around when they are back in Thailand?

He watched her as she appeared in deep thought—her face firmly planted against the partly open window staring out at the landscape flashing by. He never tired of watching her, mesmerised by her soft wavy hair— the way it curled around her swanlike neck. *What it would feel like lying back in her arms with his face nestled in the soft tresses? How could they marry if they both live on opposite sides of the globe? Where is all of this heading?* He pondered.

Paddington Station was crowded and they needed to find the train going to Heathrow Airport. Ruby was overwhelmed by the hustle and bustle with so many people rushing and pushing through the crowds. It would be so easy to lose one's way here and get lost in the crowd. She became unnerved. She grabbed onto Julian's arm and let him lead the way to the right platform. She was out of breath pulling her heavy suitcase along.

'Nearly there, Pie, then only a short trip to the airport. It's good we're going to be early. Time to grab some lunch when we arrive.'

Ruby always felt safe with Julian. He appeared so confident and unafraid of change, well-organised, competent. She began thinking that he must have an Achilles heel but just hasn't seen it yet. Perhaps it was his insecurity when she turned up at The Gables with Edward. Even though it was not her fault that she got lost, she was sure Julian was trying hard to cover up his insecurity. She felt sorry for him. It seemed as though he was frightened of losing her, suffering some sort of separation anxiety. Perhaps it will become more evident in time, but for now, she just wants to focus on his good points, of which there are many, many of which are great assets for marriage.

She quietly admonished herself for thinking so, as all her life she'd decided marriage may not be for her. Ruby had been strongly influenced by the stories her mother told her about her narcissistic father who took his own life. The stories about his cruelty, his abuse towards her mother. Initially, she couldn't understand why she had remarried, but Lyon, Ruby's step-father who had adopted her, turned out to be an honourable and respectable man. He was the father Ruby had never known, a man full of self-sacrificial love and compassion, who would never hurt a fly. He'd instilled in her a new-found interest in men.

'Rubes, you always seem to be so far away. What are you thinking about?'

'Nothing of importance— just reminiscing about the interesting experiences I've had here, especially in Devon,' she said, quickly hiding the secrets of her heart.

'We have to get off here … don't forget your hat on the seat next to you.'

The check-in seemed to take forever and Ruby had worn the wrong shoes which were uncomfortable to stand in.

'I wish I had worn my trainers as I usually do when I travel and just didn't think this time.'

'We're nearly through then we can grab a bite to eat and head off to the departure lounge. You won't need to stand any longer.'

Julian was mistaken. They had to walk the length of the airport then go up the next level to the food courts. Finally, they sat down to a substantial Thai green curry.

'I've missed the lovely healthy food we were served up at Rainbow Haven. It was always so fresh and nutritious. For Ruby, Rainbow Haven had been like home.

'You're right, me too. English food does have a reputation for being rich and stodgy. But I must admit, our chef does a pretty good job of providing an upmarket menu full of healthy options, I might add.'

Ruby nodded in agreement.

'Let's get to gate 28 and sit down and relax. Do you want to buy any paperbacks before we jump on the plane Ruby?'

'No thanks, I want to write in my diary. I've lots of catching up to do about my stay in Devon.'

Ruby loved to write, in fact, she had quite a flair for it and had won a few writing awards at the university for English literature, especially creative writing.

As they sat waiting for the departure gate to open, Julian took Ruby's hand in his. 'It feels so natural you being by my side, Ruby. I'm so glad you supported me through the aftermath of my mother's death and helped out at The Gables. I'm very grateful,' he said as he leaned over, putting an arm around her shoulders and affectionately kissing her on the lips. An old man sitting next to them looked up and smiled with a twinkle in his eye. Ruby felt a little embarrassed by Julian's sudden public display of affection but quickly warmed to his embrace.

'How long do you think you'll stay back in Rayong? Are you going to keep the position on after all?'

'Only if you stay there with me. It'll never be any good if you aren't there. I've got so used to your company, Rubes, I really value it.'

'Oh, that's nice— it's good to know I'm appreciated. I'll stay on as long as Mum and Dad can manage without me.'

'Well, if not, they'll have to employ someone else I expect.'

'It's not that easy. The kind of people we want working at Peace Haven demands special character and personality traits. It isn't just a job, it's a ministry or a calling if you like.'

'Just like Rainbow Haven has been for me and the staff who work there like Gamon, Isra, and Rolando. That's why I'm going back, as they can't so easily replace me,' said Julian.

Ruby sat there thinking what a dilemma they were in, as they each felt that their particular ministry was God-given, a calling, and one they could not so easily relinquish. What will they do? How could their relationship progress in such a complex situation? It troubled Ruby, and unbeknown to her, it concerned Julian too, but they must walk by faith and not by sight, no matter what, Ruby kept telling herself.

***

The long haul from London to Bangkok was tiring and they were travelling "cattle class" as Julian put it. There was

141

no elbow room for Ruby to write in her diary comfortably and she felt uneasy that the woman to her right could probably see what she was writing. She gave up and took out a paperback she'd purchased in Devon and started reading.

At Bangkok airport, there were more long queues. Having waited for around twenty minutes at the baggage claim, Ruby felt reluctant to get into a queue to go through customs. She remembered the terrible event she had experienced when she travelled to Malaysia with Kate and had the drugs planted in her backpack. She shuddered at the memory and thought what a breeze Julian had been to travel with instead of that awful Rick whom she and Kate were stuck with.

They were relieved to get through customs and to be able to head for a taxi to the hotel. Ruby just wanted to sleep as she found travelling exhausting and realised after all this time that she didn't really enjoy being on the move all the time.

Julian had booked two separate single rooms in the Orchadia Hotel near the airport for the night.

The hotel was not too expensive, though it did appear so. Especially with the granite floor that shone under the light of the chandeliers and a huge upmarket reception area with bellboys who carried the bags to their rooms.

They were surprised to have two rooms with a view overlooking the city, and the swimming pool below surrounded by palm trees.

Julian popped his head through Ruby's bedroom door to make sure she was happy with her room.

'It's great, no road noise—must be double glazing,' she said.

'Maybe triple, it's so quiet. Once you have settled in, how about we go down for a hot spa before they close the pool.'

'Sure, I have my bathing suit somewhere in my suitcase, I'll have a look.'

'Just tap on my door when you're ready.'

The spa surroundings were very tropical with large ferns and pretty flowering succulents around a large wooden tub which got emptied each night.

Chapter Twenty-Two

Julian couldn't believe the sight of Ruby in her beautiful full bathing suit with a low cut back and high in the leg. It revealed her toned, trim figure and he noticed she still had the strong suntan she had acquired the summer before. It was obvious she had been an athlete in her youth. He tried hard not to stare, as he took his faith seriously and prized his celibacy before marriage. But he was just human and kept reminding himself in these situations that he would be abnormal not to feel this way. He deliberately tried to distract himself, in case Ruby was made to feel uncomfortable. He'd been warned about getting into situations like this because of the danger of temptation, but they had no choice when travelling. He had so much respect for Ruby that he was sure he would not try anything inappropriate with her.

'Don't you fall asleep, Ruby... it's very easy to in here, especially after we ate so late. We shouldn't really stay in any longer than twenty minutes.'

As they sat back relaxing in the ambience of the pool surrounded by small palm trees, letting their weary muscles soak up the soft hot water, Julian was suddenly distracted. Something on Ruby's upper back caught his eye. Was it a tattoo? He quickly averted his eyes in order to not embarrass her. He imagined how soft her skin would be to touch and quickly changed his thinking.

Ruby turned over, stretching out like a cat exposing the full length of her long back. Julian was right, there was something, but it was not a tattoo. Instead, it was a thick scar the size of a golf ball behind her right shoulder blade. Dare he ask her about it? He felt tempted to rub her back, to soothe her, then stopped.

Ruby was feeling self-conscious, as she got out of the pool, aware that Julian had quickly scanned her youthful slender body.

'I'll meet you outside the changing rooms. Feel like watching a movie downstairs before you turn in?'

'I'm sorry, Julian ... I'm really done in and need to get some sleep. Thanks though.' She had second thoughts about putting herself in temptation's way.

She stood at the window of her ninth-story room dazzled by the lights of the surrounding hotels and shops. She thought of Julian in the adjoining bedroom and realised that if she hadn't been so resolute in keeping her faith, she could easily have weakened.

***

They were both glad they decided to stay overnight in Bangkok after the long haul from London. The train to Rayong was not that full and their carriage was almost empty for a change. Ruby was looking forward to seeing her friends at Rainbow Haven again, especially Gamon and Isra. She had received a few letters from Gamon while she was staying in Devon and it appeared that her relationship with Rolando had become serious, and they were both managing Rainbow Haven well without Julian or Ruby's parents.

But if they were all managing so well, where would Ruby fit in, she asked herself.

Julian found his chance as he sat close to Ruby on the train. 'Did you sleep well after the spa? I certainly did.' He held her hand and waited a few minutes as he was building up the nerve to ask her about the scar.

'Yes, I did thanks, I was so relaxed. My back had been aching quite a bit. I was so stiff from all the sitting I expect.'

Julian had observed that since they had first met, now and then she would put her hand over her right shoulder and massage it slightly, as though she was in pain.

'I hope you don't mind me asking, but is the sore shoulder from some kind of injury ... I ... um ... I couldn't help noticing a scar where you keep rubbing your shoulder.' He tensed with apprehension.

'Oh that ... I forgot about my scar.' She had a moment of silence, as if in deep thought about how to answer the question.

'You're right, it's an old injury. Gives me trouble now and then, especially when sitting for long periods. The spa certainly helped though. I should grab one more often.'

Julian noticed she didn't offer more information and felt reluctant to intrusively pry it out of her. After another period of silence, she opened up, to his surprise.

'I'll tell you about the injury, but it means delving into my past and dredging up things I've left buried for years, painful things.'

'Oh, please, don't do that for my benefit, not if it makes you feel uncomfortable.'

'No, I want to. It'll be of benefit to us both if we're to have a serious relationship.' She tried to swallow the lump in her throat.

'You see, I didn't come to know God until I was in my last year at university. My mother often told me Bible stories and shared her faith, but I had no personal revelation of God or personal encounter. I tried to get it by osmosis through other people and then gave up. Early in my university years, when I was about nineteen, I got into a bad relationship with a man ten years my senior. He took me away from the church, just as I began searching for faith and still very vulnerable. My mother warned me against the relationship as she had also had first-hand experience with such a man, namely my own father who turned out to be a misogynist. I ignored her and felt that she was over-reacting due to her own experiences.'

Julian felt taken aback by this confession. He didn't know whether he wanted her to tell him the rest but if they want a future together, they shouldn't have any secrets between them, nothing that will raise its ugly head years down the track. He urged her on.

'I fell madly in love with this man, seeing him as a sort of father figure I suppose. I clung to him for security and one night we slept together, but not intentionally on my part. He filled me up with cheap wine and as I hadn't grown up with alcohol, it went straight to my head and we ended up in bed. When I woke the next morning, hung over and sick, the worse thing was that I was horrified at what I had done, breaching my own strong values and I felt cheap. I wanted to end the relationship there and then, as I felt he'd taken advantage and did not respect me. It filled me with deep self-loathing and shame.'

Julian reached out and took her hand. The pain in her contorted face said it all.

'That's good. Did you just walk away?'

'When I told him I never wanted to see him again he was furious and in a rage picked up a large glass and threw it hard at me, leaving a deep gash in my back. I dressed quickly and fled, blood dripping through my blouse.'

'What did your folks say about all this, I suppose they wanted to throttle him?'

'I was flatting with friends near the university who took me to the local doctor to get help. It needed a lot of stitches. My parents never knew about this until years later. They were very supportive, especially my Mum who, of course, had experienced abuse from my father. Soon after that I turned to God and haven't looked back.'

Julian reminded Ruby of a favourite scripture he'd once given her.

'But Jesus said to him, No one, having put his hand to the plough, and looking back, is fit for God's Kingdom. You did the right thing and mustn't beat yourself up over the incident. God is a God of second chances and he wants to give you hope and a future. In fact, he is the God of infinite second chances.'

That's what Ruby loved about Julian, always a soft word of encouragement without judgement to give someone—precious quality to have in someone you love.

Ruby never appeared hard or bitter. God's grace was with her. Julian rested his head on her shoulder. They'd formed a close spiritual bond. It wasn't so long ago that his own heart had been broken. He was overjoyed that they'd found each other.

***

As the train pulled into the platform, Ruby spotted Gamon and Isra waving with beaming smiles. They appeared excited to see them return.

Ruby gathered together her luggage, singling out the small packages—gifts she'd purchased in Devon for her two friends. They half squeezed Ruby to death with excitement. 'We've so much to tell you. Lani has even prepared something special for you for dinner tonight.'

Julian drove to Rainbow Haven slowly, listening to the women as they chatted incessantly, catching up on all their news.

When they arrived at Rainbow Haven, Isra took hold of Ruby's hand, leading her back to the residence.

There were many new faces at the home, amongst them some new children. Ruby noticed how healthy they appeared, in spite of their traumatic experiences. Rainbow Haven was a true haven for them.

She slipped away to her room soon after dinner and collapsed on her bed. The sudden impact of the hot, humid tropical climate after being in England was taxing. She preferred a cooler climate and found adjusting a lot more difficult this time.

She pulled the mosquito net around her. The night was still except for the pounding of her heart against her eardrums. Before long, oblivion had found her.

***

'Rolando— come and sit down. I hear you've put me out of a job here, mate. You've certainly been doing wonders running the centre.'

'Nah, it was Gamon mostly. She knows the ropes more than I do. I suppose we've been running it together. We're a pretty good team.'

Julian poured a glass of fresh pineapple juice and handed it to him.

'Fresh juice?'

'Yes, thanks.' He took a few loud gulps. 'So ... what's on the agenda?'

'We're preparing for another raid in Pattaya. This brothel is full of children—boys and girls who are rented out to tourists, some as young as six. It smells of a local paedophile ring.'

Julian hated this part of the job, extracting children from the hands of paedophiles. It took all the self-control he could muster to keep himself from throttling them when they raided the buildings.

Ruby found the raids heart-breaking, especially when they discovered children who were stressed and mentally damaged. Some children never recovered.

'Ruby is coming with us this time. She's really good with the children and has a great rapport with our clinical

149

psychologist. The little ones seem to attach themselves to her. She can get them aside and distract them while we deal with the police.'

'That's a great idea. We've several beds available now that the university students have moved out into the student residence.'

'I'll ask Gamon if she could accompany Ruby too as we'll need her to translate for the some of the children.'

***

The helicopter circled over the thatched rooftops of the pole houses in a rural area near the red light district. The police filled two large blacked out vans which rallied around the helicopter in the field where it landed. Ruby and Gamon went with Julian and Phillipe, the policeman in another vehicle. The police and welfare workers prepared the helicopter to receive the children. They would then be quickly flown out of Pattaya to the south of Rayong and transported to Rainbow Haven.

The building was in a filthy, dark back street with stray dogs, and rats running through the gutters. There was a hefty security guard standing watch at the front of the building. Phillipe spoke to his police colleagues standing next to the helicopter.

'Right team, here's the plan. Julian and I are to go inside first. We'll have mini video cameras fitted under our clothing and once they offer me the rent-boys and Phillipe catches it on video, the rest of you will raid the building. The children will be quickly taken in the vans to the helicopter in the field and flown out of there. Let's go!'

As he arrived at the top of the stairs in a darkened room, Julian stopped short, his throat muscles tightened with fury. An obese, sleazy character offered him the young boys who were no older than seven or eight.

'You want a boy? You have one boy or pay more you get two, three boys. You can buy or rent—you pay more to buy.'

As Julian approached the offender, he almost choked on the fishy stench emanating from the man's mouth. His body reeked even worse.

'Sure, I take the three little ones in the corner. They experienced?'

'Yes, Mister, they do special tricks for you mister, very experienced.' The boys cringed. Their eyes widened as their overseer approached them. They cowered in the corner of the room while holding on tight to each other. Not only fearful of the strange men who had been viewing them, but more so of their custodian.

'Your friend there want boys too?' He pointed at Phillipe who had been standing in the background stealthily filming the transaction with a hidden camera. As the fat man grabbed the boys by the arms, roughly yanking them onto their feet to meet their fake buyer, the armed police stormed through the door. A policewoman quickly bustled the boys downstairs out of the way while the brothel owner was arrested along with three other men found in the building. Ruby and Gamon were waiting outside in a van waiting to receive the boys along with four small girls they had found locked in another room— girls no older than five were found in a dirty space not much bigger than a wardrobe. They were promptly evacuated to safety.

It was a tragic scene. The traumatised children were taken away quickly to the helicopter in the field and airlifted to a hospital near Rayong. A couple of the girls sat trembling, clinging on to Ruby and the two children's nurses on board. Ruby also couldn't steady her own hands. Her throat had dried up and she had difficulty swallowing. Would she be able to see this mission through?

Gamon kept telling the children in Thai that they were safe and had been rescued. Ruby was close to tears, overwhelmed with compassion for these victims of unbelievable abuse.

'What happens now, Gamon?' she whispered. 'How long will they stay in the hospital?'

'They'll undergo tests for any infections or diseases they may have and then receive a psychological assessment to see how damaged they are. They can then ascertain what programs they'll need for rehabilitation.'

'Are they coming to us at Rainbow Haven then?'

'Once they're cleared, if they don't need ongoing medical treatment. Some children we've rescued have been HIV positive or had hepatitis.'

Chapter Twenty-Three

Ruby felt her pulse in her temples pounding when she thought of what damage the evil predators had done to these children. She'd already witnessed the plight of several of the residents at Rainbow Haven who still required ongoing psychological therapy and those who were made sterile by sexually transmitted infections.

As they arrived at the hospital, Phillipe and Julian were waiting for Ruby and Gamon. A medical team was there to receive the children. Ruby promised them she would come and visit them and they seemed to really take to her well.

'Don't worry Ruby... they'll be well looked after. They have a special medical team in the children's hospital and there are motherly sorts, volunteers who visit them every day until they leave.'

Ruby wasn't sure she had the stomach for all this. She secretly regretted agreeing to accompany this raid. She would rather have just visited the children in the hospital once they'd been admitted than see the fear and panic on their faces.

***

Ruby put on her night attire and turned out the light—her body tense and aching and eyelids heavy with fatigue. If only she could soak in a hot bath with special salts like she used to do back home. That would fix her tense neck and low back muscles. Now she couldn't relax and fall asleep. The frightful images of the children kept invading her mind. Especially the way Julian had described the mental state of the rescued boys, the look of terror on their faces and the grotesque appearance of the dirty, bloated man with body odour who terrified the children. The little girls too, locked in the room emaciated and gaunt, with faces as white as a sheet. She started to pray for them, just as she prayed for all the residents of Rainbow Haven when they arrived, visualising them healed with smiling faces and healthy bodies. Praying helped her fall asleep.

The sound of birds in the trees outside her room on waking reminded her she was back in Rainbow Haven. She pulled on her blue cotton dressing gown and stumbled sleepily towards the window. Downstairs in the garden, she could see some of the children who'd been in the program for nearly a year. They were full of energy, healthy and happy—chasing each other around the garden as though they'd never endured a bad moment in their lives. But they, too, had been rescued from a similar situation and were on the road to recovery. Her face lit up seeing them happy. She could see the hand of God in their lives as they were nurtured into recovery. There was hope for last night's children too.

There was a knock on the door. 'Are you awake Rubes? I thought I saw you at your window. Can I come in?' Julian poked his head slowly through the door.

'Yeah, come on in.' She pushed her hand through her hair, as she hadn't yet combed it. 'Have you had anything to eat yet?'

'No, I was on my way to the dining room.'

'Well, if you wait a few minutes, I'll make us some coffee and toast. I have some bananas too.'

As they sat on the tiny veranda outside her humble room, Ruby appeared subdued, almost downcast.

'What's wrong, Cherry Pie? Are you okay?'

'No, not really. I'm still trying to come to terms with the events of yesterday—can't keep the images of those poor children out of my head. It's the first raid I've been on and it was horrific.'

'Yeah, but they've been rescued! Surely that should put a smile on your face.'

'I know, but I can't help thinking how petrified they looked and how damaged they are. Their childhood is wrecked now. The thing that upsets me most is knowing that this is a drop in the ocean compared to the thousands of children who are suffering like this and never get rescued.'

'That's why Rescue Net exists, and other organisations like us who do good work like this all around the world. There are many rescues going on all the time now and Thailand is in the process of trying to stamp out the child sex trade completely. They'll all be discovered eventually.'

Ruby thought how ironic it was to be working in a five-star hotel in the Devonshire countryside, catering to the wealthy middle-class tourists. Then finding herself in a dark backstreet, gathering children who were starving and beaten, from a brothel full of paedophiles. Most people who enjoy their comfortable, materialistic lives wouldn't even know this existed. These children are the forgotten ones.

Ruby realised that Rescue Net was a special ministry, a kind of divine "calling". But is this where God wanted her? She wondered if she was really cut out for this work.

'Mmm, this coffee sure is good.'

'I grind the beans myself. One of my little luxuries, my coffee grinder... I bought it in Cornwall.'

'My favourite breakfast—freshly ground coffee and toast with marmalade.'

'Julian licked his fingers. Mmm. Orange, isn't it? Where did you get it?'

'Mum sends it over to me. She makes it herself. I'll ask her to send you a jar.'

'Let's get out of here today and go for a drive to Rayong Botanical Gardens. They have a cafe there too.'

'Sure ... sounds great.' Ruby had clear memories of her first date with Julian at the botanical gardens in Bangkok. She remembered Julian strutting along all dressed to the nines for her, very debonair looking. She was so impressed that day— he was such a gentleman and he had never let her down since.

'I wonder if there are geese at this one. Remember the ones that chased us?'

Ruby dressed in her favourite sky blue chenille skirt and white cotton blouse and posed in front of her mirror. She pulled on her walking shoes—a pair of white plimsolls purchased in Devon. She was going on a date.

Julian waited for her outside in the land rover. When she jumped in alongside him, the sweet fragrance of his strong aftershave caught her breath. She grinned. *He's overdone it again.*

It was another sunny day—the sky a radiant blue. It wasn't scorching hot weather, but gently warming.

As Ruby stepped out of the vehicle, Julian approached her and reached out to take her hand. He seemed extra attentive today.

'Come this way, Rubes ... over there is where the more exotic plants are. Succulents with huge unusual flowers.'

Ruby loved that way Julian shared her passion with the outdoors and wildlife. And even though he didn't overtly show it, inside he was soft and gentle as a lamb.

They stood photographing the exotic flowers and walked on further where they could hear the sound of water.

'There's a mini waterfall here enclosed in an enormous aviary with rare and tropical birds. There are even Bird of Paradise flowers.'

He took her hand again. Ruby felt secure when he did that, especially when he appeared so confident and strong, which was most of the time.

As they approached the waterfall, Julian asked a passer-by to take their photo. He leaned into Ruby with his arm around her, as though posing for something special.

'Thanks very much,' he said to the woman. She was Vietnamese and couldn't speak a word of English. She nodded and walked on flashing a broad smile amidst a set of broken front teeth.

Ruby looked at the photo produced by the Polaroid camera. She couldn't help notice how attractive Julian looked in his navy shorts and a white tee shirt, revealing his toned chest muscles. 'We look like a good match, don't you think?' He teased, kissing her gently on the lips.

They sat on a wooden bench near the pond and watched a pair of swans caressing each other with their long necks.

'Look at that, Rubes! The swans have formed a heart with their necks if you look side on.'

The elegant birds were sitting in the middle of the pond facing each other with their beaks touching, which formed a heart shape with their necks.

'Do you know that they're very loyal to their mates and they mate for life?' he said, flushing slightly.'

Ruby was quite taken aback by this sudden display of sentimentality from Julian. It was becoming obvious to her that he was a sensitive soul somewhat like her. She felt uncomfortable with his subtle reference to a life mate.

'I suppose we should be getting back. Gamon wanted to have a meeting with us before dinner tonight. She has something important to tell us.' Ruby felt guilty for breaking the spell of a dreamy, romantic, sunny afternoon in the gardens.

'Oh, that's right. I wonder what she wants to see us about.'

Ruby wondered if her friend had decided to leave Rainbow Haven. She felt a little anxious, although she had thought of moving on herself soon.

Gamon was waiting outside the meeting room. 'Hi, you two. Come on inside. I've some cake and tea for you both.'

'Sure, what on earth are you up to now Gamon?' Ruby looked across and saw Rolando standing there with a huge grin on his face.

'Oh no, looks like a bit of a set up to me.' Julian winked at Ruby.

They sat around the decorative Rotan coffee table eating the banana and coconut cake Gamon placed on the table. 'Come on, please both test my new recipe,' she said, handing them each a plate with a slice of cake.

Julian gobbled his piece quickly, washing it down with pineapple juice.

'Sure is good. Thanks, Gamon.'

'Right, who's going to speak first?' Julian thought he would prize it out of them before they change their minds.

'We have some good news for you and we need to ask you a favour also.' Gamon stood up, handing the plate of cake around again. She carefully separated the remaining slices, keeping her focus on the shredded coconut about to fall off the iced cake and handed the plate around. Taking her seat again, she nodded at Rolando a few times.

'Well, it's time for some more changes folks. We want you to celebrate our engagement with us. We are getting married in June this year.'

'Wow! That's great news Gamon!' Ruby wrapped her arms around Gamon, squeezing the breath out of her. Gamon gasped. Ruby turned and grabbed hold of Rolando in the same way.

'Thanks, Ruby', said Rolando. 'The thing is ... we want to go to Canada for our honeymoon. I have relatives there who want to meet Gamon. But we're wondering if you can do without us here for a month?'

'I'm sure we could work something out. Don't you worry about that, Rolando? You two are overdue for a good holiday. There's Isra and also Adam, the youth worker you've been training … I hear he's very capable.'

'Do you have a date for the wedding? And what about a venue?' Ruby had her head in her diary.

'I was going to ask Pastor Michael from our Christian Fellowship to marry us. Maybe we can hire the big band kiosk in the botanical gardens as a venue.'

Ruby had a quick word in Julian's ear.

'Why not have it here in our gardens? The flowers will all be out then and we can ask some of the older girls if they'd like to help prepare food.'

'Really? Would that be ok? What do you think?' Her glance darted at Rolando who was busy tucking into his second large piece of Gamon's cake.

Ruby couldn't believe that Gamon would soon be a married woman. The young girl who came to Rainbow Haven battered and traumatised had become healed and restored. Her life had been completely turned around, but Ruby wondered how she could just put a past like that out of mind, out of sight. It would take a lot of faith, which Gamon certainly had. She was happy for her friend, seeing the enormous restoration taking place in her life. Ruby also believed that Rolando was heaven sent and would take good care of her.

***

June came far too fast for Gamon. There was so much to organise before the wedding in two weeks. She was grateful to have the support of Ruby and Julian and to be able to have the wedding in the gardens at Rainbow Haven. She saw them both as family now, but there were some greater changes in the air for them all.

'Hi, Ruby, thanks for leaving the leaflet in my pigeonhole about the dresses. The dress-maker sounds really reasonable. You said she'll see us tomorrow?'

'Yes, you'll have to get onto it Gamon, as she needs time to make it. I look forward to seeing her samples. She has them displayed on mannequins.'

'Oh, thanks, Ruby, you're such a good friend, I really appreciate your help.' She placed a long, slender arm around Ruby's waist and they continued to discuss the wedding dress.

Chapter Twenty-Four

The big day came quickly. The residents at Rainbow Haven were all invited to the wedding. Gamon chose two of the young boys as page boys and Ruby and Isra as bridesmaids. Julian was asked to be Rolando's best man. There was an atmosphere of excitement in the garden as garlands of frangipani, gardenia, white roses and tiny slipper orchids were ornately placed on the long white tables covered with stiff white linen. Even the wooden benches in the park-like gardens were decorated with flowers. The sky was a brilliant blue providing an artist's background for the flowers. The gentle breeze kept the outside temperature comfortable instead of humid and sticky.

Half a dozen women who'd been trained in catering were elected by Gamon to prepare the food and serve it. Lyon and Cherie had gifted the funds for the wedding meal as Gamon and Rolando were seen as extended family.

Phillipe arrived with his friends, a small musical group who agreed to play background music.

Julian walked up to Ruby poking her in the ribs playfully. 'Well, Pie, what do you think? Do we have the perfect setting for your friend's wedding?'

'It couldn't be better, and I think you're quite the romantic, aren't you? A lot of men wouldn't notice these things.'

Rolando looked the part in his white suit with a pink orchid in his buttonhole, contrasted by his thick, shiny black hair. He waited next to Pastor Michael for his bride to arrive, clasping his fingers together tightly. Small beads of perspiration appeared on his forehead. His stare was fixed at the door to the gardens where Gamon would soon be walking towards him. The music ensemble started to play a popular piece of music, a favourite of both of them, "When I Fall in Love" by Michael Crawford. As Gamon walked into the garden, Rolando was mesmerised by the sight of this beautiful woman dressed in a delicate, white, French lace dress, showing off her elegant curves and tiny waist. She looked a picture— unreal. He regained his composure as Pastor Michael checked his readiness.

At the ceremony, Julian noticed Ruby had tears in her eyes. She looked away. What was behind the tears— joy or sadness?

Gamon threw the bouquet up into the air in traditional style. It happened to be caught by Ruby who stood blushing with embarrassment at the inference of several bystanders. Especially Julian who approached her to test her reaction.

'I think it's not very spiritual really, people believing the bouquet is some kind of talisman,' Ruby muttered quietly to Julian.

'Who knows, maybe it's God's will.' He gently poked her in the ribs.

Ruby began wondering why there was all of this reference to marriage from Julian, especially when he'd never actually proposed. Perhaps he is one of those men who talk about it but never commit. And she is not going to push it either. If it's meant to be, it'll come from him at the right time. Now isn't the right time with everything up in the air, that's for sure.

***

Rainbow Haven happened to be unusually quiet while the honeymooners were away.

'It's almost as though it were divine intervention,' Ruby said to Isra as she helped her and a few others clear up the hall the next day.

'I know what you mean—no raids in the pipeline at present and our residents are mostly settled in now.'

'I was rather surprised to hear at our meeting that Phillipe had applied for the role of coordinator at Rainbow Haven. You weren't there Isra so you may have missed the news.'

'I heard from Gamon that he'd accepted the position. It's marvellous! I really like him. He seems so brave and strong, yet gentle and kind.'

'You mean like a gentle giant? I couldn't think of anyone who could be more suited to that position. He's also very experienced. Apparently, he has an award from the United Nations for his work combatting human trafficking in Thailand as well as cyber-crime involving paedophiles.'

'I can't wait to have him join our team. When will that be Ruby?' Isra was inadvertently revealing the obvious crush she had on Phillipe.

'Julian said he's starting the week after Gamon and Rolando get back so that they can orientate him.'

'Ruby ... Is Julian really leaving us? I mean— is he going back home to England again? I just heard that Phillipe is taking over his role to free him up to move on.'

'Who told you that ... Gamon?'

'Phillipe mentioned that Julian may want to move on and that's why he's taking over his role in case he does go.'

'Goodness—word certainly gets around here in a hurry. I honestly don't think that Julian knows himself where he's headed. He had an offer from Lyon to help out at my parent's holistic retreat in New Zealand, but who knows what he might decide. Let's just wait and see. Ruby tried to put it out of her mind.

***

'Ruby, your Mum is on the phone.'

'Is everything alright? She instinctively felt something was amiss.

'I'm not sure ... she didn't say much to me, just wanted to speak to you.' Julian handed her the phone, hesitated then walked away to give her some privacy.

'Mum, how are you? Good to hear from you—sorry I haven't written to you lately since I've been back from England. It has been pretty busy since we got back.'

'Yes, I know. Julian wrote to Lyon about the last raid and the children they rescued. It all seems to be under control with your staff levels I hear.'

'Pretty well, except Gamon and Rolando are in Canada for their honeymoon for a month.'

'The thing is, Ruby, we need you back home now. Lyon has had an accident, but not too serious. He fell off a ladder cleaning the roof gutters in a storm and broke his leg. I'm having to run the lodge and continue my appointments at the women's refuge in Cromwell Mead. We need your help as we can't easily find experienced staff to fill in.'

'Oh, no, poor Dad. Is he in pain?'

'Not much, but his leg is in plaster above the knee and he gets very tired. He's also had some mild concussion from his head injury.'

Ruby started to feel guilty that she'd stayed away for so long, letting her parents run the lodge on their own. Annie and Murray, who are retired, still work part-time, though they are ageing.

'We'll pay for your tickets to fly home. Sorry, Ruby, but we really do need your help at the moment.'

Ruby knew her mother wouldn't ask her to come home unless it was a desperate situation, and she couldn't leave her in the lurch.

'What about Rainbow Haven? We're going to be without Gamon and Rolando for a month.'

'I'll talk to Julian to see what arrangements he can make with the rest of the staff while they're away. It's only for a month, I'm sure they'll manage and there are no raids planned at present.'

Ruby's heart sank. She was in a dilemma. She didn't want to let her mother down. On the other hand, she was afraid that if she left Julian behind in Thailand, she might never see him again. What if someone else walks into his life, especially now when they have become like soul mates.

'Okay Mum, I'll put Julian on— hold on.'

Ruby reluctantly went up to Julian to break the news. She watched his face drop when he was talking to Cherie. He discussed with her the staffing situation and listened to some instructions which he took graciously.

'Thanks, Cherie, give my regards to Lyon. Tell him I'll be keeping him up to date. I'll make sure that Ruby gets on the plane, don't you worry.'

Ruby felt despondent when Julian came off the phone. He acted aloof, reserved, as though the news of her having to fly home didn't sway him.

'Come on, Ruby, let's get back. We can talk about this later and make plans— come on.' He took her hand and led her through to the dining room where the team was cleaning up the hall.

When the rest of the group dispersed, Ruby left quietly without Julian noticing. She wandered into the garden and sat on the bench under the weeping cherry tree, pondering the day's events. Why do things go wrong, just when everything is going smoothly?

'God— help me to make the right decision now.' she prayed. 'Lead me and guide me, Lord, as I don't know where I am meant to be right now.'

Ruby sat with her head in her hands, feeling a little down. Since her relationship with Julian had developed into something serious, she took it for granted she had a future with him. But now it seemed to her that all her hopes and dreams had hit a brick wall and she couldn't understand why.

Chapter Twenty-Five

Ruby hadn't seen that Julian had wandered into the garden. She sat slumped forward with her arms resting on her thighs, looking at the ground with a dejected expression on her face. When she heard his footsteps, she quickly pulled herself together, hoping he didn't notice. He sat down beside her and pulled her close to him. She relaxed back in his arms, feeling comforted.

'Don't worry, Rubes I know you're upset about this. We'll work something out. Perhaps when things have settled down, I could come over to you.'

Ruby couldn't believe her ears. Was he meaning he might want to come and live in Cromwell Mead?

'You mean for a visit, or to work? You would have to give up your position here.'

'Would that be such a bad thing though? I'm sure Gamon and Rolando can run Rainbow Haven and Rescue Net quite adequately with the staff we have. No one is indispensable, Ruby. Sooner or later your parents won't be able to manage Peace Haven either.'

Ruby wondered where Julian was heading with this.

'Lyon had a chat with me when he was last out here and asked if I might be interested in using my skills to come and work in Peace Haven as a men's crisis counsellor. I couldn't see that far ahead at the time, as I had to go back and sort out my mother's affairs.'

'Is that what you're thinking ... I mean coming to Cromwell Mead?' Ruby eyes widened, her well-shaped eyebrows forming two arches in her forehead.

'I can't at this point in time until Gamon and Rolando are back. But once that's sorted … the world's our oyster,' he said, squeezing Ruby's hand.

She was in a quandary, wondering what he meant by that. All of a sudden, a commotion in the tree above them distracted her. As she looked at the top of the tree, she saw two noisy, green pigeons caressing each other, running up and down the branch together as though they were playing a game.

'Look at that, just like the swans at the botanical gardens. Maybe it's some sort of sign for us, Cherry Pie.'

Ruby was thinking that he hadn't used that endearment for a while, and usually only when he was confident of her devotion to him.

'I've been thinking.' He seemed lost for words all of a sudden. 'I was wondering what your thoughts are on settling down and having a family. I mean … we never discuss it. If we are to make a commitment in the future, it is important to discuss these things first, don't you think? In case we have differing agendas.'

Ruby felt a lump in her throat. It was the kind of conversation she dreaded, the thought of a lifelong commitment, yet deep down she longed for stability and companionship. It scared her too.

'What kind of things do you want to discuss?' She didn't make it easy for the poor man who was insightful enough to sense her discomfort.

'Well … things like having a family and staying at home with children— I mean that some girls don't like the idea of being a stay-at-home Mum.'

'Oh, I see.' Ruby clamped her teeth over her bottom lip. 'You're wanting to work out whether I'm breeding material or not,' she blurted. Her tone half joking and half serious almost sounded offensive.

'Oh sorry, Pie, I've put it the wrong way! Put my big foot in it again. What I mean is … I'd like to settle down and have two or three children someday, with the right woman of course. I was hoping we might be on the same page. What do you think? Are you wanting a family too?'

'Yes, I've thought about it, but I don't believe a woman has to be barefoot and pregnant and give up her career. I'd like to think that the gifts and talents God has given me are to be used for the rest of my life.'

'What do you mean? What kind of career do you see yourself pursuing in the future?' Julian stiffened, waiting for her answer.

'I'd like to be like my Mum. She has spent her whole life as a social worker, specialising in the restoration of abused and traumatised women, even when she was raising me. My grandparents helped out when they could when Mum when to university, and when they couldn't, she placed me in the university childcare centre. When I was older, she went to work at Peace Haven as a counsellor and helped run the lodge there with Annie and Murray. She also ran groups and did personal counselling at the Women's Refuge in Cromwell Mead. She told me it was a ministry, a divine calling. Well, I think I have that calling too.'

'But you were a teenager when your mother did that.'

'No, she was working as a social worker in Winton Abbott when I was at primary school. She was passionate about her work, and was also a wonderful, loving mother.'

'But it would be different if you had two or three children. Not so easy to pursue a career then.'

Ruby started to feel some irritation at his assumption that she would have to give up her passion to look after their children and be denied the opportunity to do God's work as she saw it. As though this was his reason for marrying, just to have someone to bear his children and stay home, no longer giving her the opportunity to follow her heart as he does in his ministry.

'So you think that if a woman marries and has children, she must give up her passion or God-given calling. That sounds sexist to me Julian.' She was demoralised. The pink cloud of romance had a chink in it and she could sense a dark rain cloud descending. But she was determined to talk this out, as this conversation could make or break their relationship.

'Rubes, love, I think you have the wrong end of the stick, I really do. I think you and I are both passionate about the same kind of ministry like this one here, and I think it is something we could pursue together... I mean for the future. We could both work with a family if we decide to have one. What do you think?'

Ruby could see the concern on his face, that he may have altered her perception of him.

'You mean here at Rainbow Haven ... do you want to raise a family here? Oh, Julian, I'm not so sure I want to stay in Thailand. I was just supposed to help out here temporarily after my trip to Australia.'

'No, Rubes. I'd like us both to work together at Peace Haven. I feel God is drawing us there, to take it over from your parents, just as your folks took over from Anne and Murray. Lyon told me all about it. A God-given love ministry in Cromwell Mead.'

Belle suddenly lost her despondence and showed new enthusiasm for Julian's plan.

'So what was all the reference to having a family all about Julian? You confuse me.'

'I'm sorry, Pie ... I was a bit presumptuous. I was thinking Peace Haven sounded like the perfect place to raise a family while we share the healing ministry together. We would share the responsibility of course. I didn't think otherwise.'

'You sound as though we are two dyed in the wool married people already and we haven't even discussed marriage!' She found it amusing.

'Ah, that's in the pipeline ... that's our next talk lined up.'

'Don't you think you have the cart before the horse, all this talk about family though?' Ruby shook her head with exasperation.

Julian laughed it off but realised how premature the conversation sounded. The lobster colour on his neck made its way to his cheeks.

'Come on, Rubes, let's wind this up, and make some plans. I need to write a program for Phillipe's orientation, but you and I have lots to discuss. How about we go for a meal tomorrow night at the Sweet Chilli, the little restaurant near the bridge. We can also book your air tickets at the travel agent on the way there.'

Ruby was eager to meet Julian the next day to finalise their plans for the near future. She waited for him outside his office and saw one of the staff inside talking to him. She peered conspicuously through the small window and noticed that Julian was all spruced up, looking the part again in well-coordinated attire. His grooming was always impeccable, not overly dressed, but even in his casual clothing he was always easy on the eye in. He looked her way and she quickly glanced away, aware she had been staring. The staff member walked through the door politely greeting Ruby as she passed her on her way out.

Julian had his jacket in his hand, ready to go.

'How's your day been, Rubes? I saw you go off with Isra to Briggs Enterprises. How did that go?'

'Quite sad, really. Isra and I have had a lot of involvement with some of the staff since our people have been working there. I'll miss some of them. It all seems so final ... I hate goodbyes.'

She was feeling even more upset about the heart-rending farewell to come with Julian's departure but said nothing.

When they wandered into the travel agent, a woman who was known to them both greeted them warmly. Ruby walked up to the counter stammering, 'I need to get back to my home in Cromwell Mead and I haven't got a return ticket.'

'Don't fret dear Ruby— let me see what I can do.' She picked up her phone and made a call. Within minutes she had a discounted flight organised for Auckland.

They enjoyed a leisurely walk to the café after that. Julian chose a small, cosy corner of the restaurant where there was a table for two. 'It's quiet tonight. I'll grab a menu for you, or are you going to have your regular one?' Julian had detected her sombre mood.

'You mean Pad Thai noodles with chicken? Yep— I don't feel like being adventurous tonight.'

Julian was trying to find the right moment to change the subject and talk about her leaving Thailand or more to the point when he was going to join her. He sat sipping his coconut water, watching Ruby's face.

'I've been thinking a lot about what we discussed the other day— about sharing a ministry, a healing ministry to hurting people, like those who come to Peace Haven.' He leaned over and cupped one of her hands in his.

'I prayed about it, Ruby and neither of us would have to give up our work. Missionaries all around the globe raise children while living and working amongst the poor, impoverished, and oppressed. It's a life work for husband and wife. There's no reason we can't have a shared ministry like that.'

'What are you trying to say, Julian? I don't see where you are going with this.'

'What I thought is that we could make a plan. When things are settled here and Rainbow Haven is running smoothly with the staff changes, I can come to you. We could work alongside each other after my induction at Peace Haven to see how it goes—if it really is the right direction to take and whether we have both heard from God correctly. I need to know it will work for us both. Don't you think this is the right direction to take to start with?'

'Sounds wonderful to me. That's if you're happy with your new role at Peace Haven. Mum and Dad will work alongside you, and Murray, the previous owner is still in the Trust and part of Peace Haven. He's very experienced in crisis intervention with the men in the community.'

Hearing Julian talk like this was a relief for Ruby. The furrows in her brow that had recently developed seemed to disappear as her body relaxed back into her chair.

'What I was thinking, Rubes, was that we could take it a day at a time, and if we're happy about the way things are going we could talk about taking our relationship to the next level. I'm sorry, it all sounds so clinical, but we really do have to be sure about everything ... especially if it means moving from one country to another.

Ruby bit her lip. She felt the sting of reality set in, but he was right—it would be senseless to race ahead of themselves unless they were sure they were on the right path.

'Dad mentioned you could stay in one of the bedrooms that has an ensuite and I'll be in the flat with Mum and Lyon as there is a spare bedroom in their flat.'

'Well, that's settled then. We just have to let it run its course. If we're meant to be together Ruby, it'll work out. I'll really miss you though ... come on, let's walk back now.' He took her hand as she stood up almost over-doing the attention he was showing her. Could he sense her apprehension about their impending separation?

As they walked outside in the freshening night air, he helped her drape her soft cotton shawl around her bare shoulders, covering the shoulder straps of her blue and white jacquard dress which tapered and accentuated her trim waist. He held her hand during the entire walk back to the residence, and in his usual, gentlemanly fashion, kissed her at the door and said goodnight.

Chapter Twenty-Six

The next morning, a dark cloud of sadness hovered over Ruby as Julian drove her to the airport. She recognised her feelings of separation anxiety but didn't know how to control them. The issue they had discussed in the Sweet Chilli café stayed uppermost in her mind. He had promised her he would soon come to Cromwell Mead, once Phillipe was settled into his role and Gamon and Rolando were confidently running Rainbow Haven together. She prayed silently for peace of mind so that she could let go and let God.

Next to her seat on the plane were two empty seats, which was unusual for this time of the year. She was sure they would be quickly filled, but to her delight, they remained empty—room for her elbows when reading her book, and to just sit back and be herself.

She craned her neck to see if she could see Julian waving through the observation deck where he said he would be, but slumped back disappointed when she couldn't see the area from her seat. The butterflies in her stomach returned at the thought of not being able to see her friend and companion for God only knows how long. She closed her eyes, gripping the armrests tightly, waiting for take-off.

'Excuse me, madam, but are you Ruby Preston? Do you have your passport?' The young flight attendant startled her as her thoughts were interrupted with a jolt at hearing the woman's voice.

'Sorry, I didn't mean to startle you. We've upgraded you to business class if you'd like to follow me.'

Ruby was delighted. She'd always travelled cattle class, as she called it, and could never afford business class. She was ushered into the luxurious area to be waited on hand and foot. It made her trip more interesting. She sat back like the queen of Sheba, settled in and picked up the book she had begun reading.

***

Cherie and Lyon had driven all the way to Auckland airport to meet her. Cherie was so looking forward to seeing her daughter and have her home again. As Ruby pushed her trolley towards the arrival lounge, her mother ran towards her, throwing her arms around her grown-up daughter.

'Come here, my love and give your Mum a big hug.'

Ruby looked behind her to see her father hobbling along with a huge smile, waiting in line for a hug too. He walked towards her with his leg in plaster and Ruby was surprised to see him using a walking stick. She rushed forward and threw her arms around him.

'It's so good of you both to come up to meet me. I could have taken the inter-city bus from here. I do appreciate it though.'

'Are you hungry? Or did you get enough to eat on the plane?'

'No, not yet. Yes, they did feed us, thanks.'

Cherie drove while Ruby sat in the front. Lyon took the opportunity to catnap in the back.

'We've been really busy, honestly, otherwise, I wouldn't have asked you to come home,' said Cherie.

'That's okay—I was starting to get homesick, anyway. I've been away for ages it seems.'

'Yes, and Belle and Milton at Seabird Lodge are busting to see you. They haven't seen you for years.'

'My goodness, they must be quite old now. Are they still living in that huge place? I thought they would have moved on by now to something smaller.'

'No way! They said they would have to be carried out in a box. Their two sons have built a self-contained extension for them attached to the lodge. Their son Harry is running the lodge as a Bed and Breakfast place successfully and works remotely from home for a digital company. So now Belle and Milton have some support and can stay in their home.'

'That sounds like a brilliant set up. I can't wait to catch up with them. They are like grandparents to me.'

'Well, you did spend a lot of time at Peace Haven as a young child when they were running it. They are your extended family.'

'What about their other son, Jimmy? What are Jimmy and Penny up to these days? The last time I saw them they were talking about moving down here too.'

'Yes, they moved down almost a year ago now. Jimmy has an interesting business down here. He has produced a prototype for robotic cow milking in Winton Abbot, near Cromwell Mead. Most of the large farms have purchased them and it is now a lucrative business. They have a lifestyle block so Penny can have her horses. They also help out at the Bed and Breakfast business at Seabird Lodge to give Harry and Anna a break now and then. Perhaps you could pay them a visit sometime.'

'And Annie and Murray? Are they still in Lavender Cottage?'

'Oh, yes, and they don't ever want to leave either. They still own it and help out running the lodge and caring for the chickens. Murray is our handyman still and mows the grass on the four acres we have left since we sold off the rest. He still does crisis intervention and grief counselling part-time when we need him.'

'To think that Annie and Murray first met me as a baby. That's a long time ago. The last time I saw them was when I graduated from university.

'That's right. They still work hard around the place, but it's really time they retired.'

***

Her first night at Peace Haven, Ruby had mixed feelings about being back home, especially having to leave Julian behind. As she stretched out on her bed in the room her parents had reserved for her, she kept remembering the promise Julian had made to her the evening before she had returned to New Zealand. He said he'd soon be arriving in Cromwell Mead and that she had to trust him to follow through on this. It was difficult for her to believe and she struggled to get off to sleep. She prayed for Julian's protection and for her own peace of mind.

She awakened the next morning to the sound of a familiar, heart-warming voice.

'Good morning, Ruby! It's so good to have you back home.' Annie rushed towards Ruby who stood in her lilac candlewick dressing gown on her sun-drenched veranda.

'Annie! I was going to pop over to Lavender Cottage to see you later.' Ruby embraced her old friend and was surprised to see Annie's grey hair but to Ruby, she still appeared youthful looking.

'I was busting to see you, Ruby. I can't believe my eyes— you have grown into a beautiful woman. And I hear you have a man in your life.'

'Who told you that? I haven't at the moment ... he's stuck back in Thailand at present.'

'Well, you'll just have to work hard on him. Get writing and let him know how much we need him here.'

178

'No, thanks. I think I'll leave that up to him to decide. It's between him and God to work out. I'm not into forcing my will in any situation as it never works out.'

Annie could see that Ruby felt uncomfortable talking about the subject and moved on.

'Well, you've been dearly missed here, Ruby. Once you've settled in, do come and see us at the cottage. I'll bake some of your favourite apple tarts when you come. Let me know.'

Ruby reminisced about the time her parents had stayed in Lavender Cottage when she was a young girl. She spent a lot of time chasing the chickens or the baby goat and Annie was always so kind to her.

Chapter Twenty-Seven

Two weeks had gone by and no word from Julian. What was even worse was Annie continually asking Ruby if she'd heard from him, until Ruby asked her to stop. She kept wondering if he had second thoughts about coming out to join her, then she remembered the promise he'd made to her just before she flew out from Thailand. She gave in and decided she just had to be patient and trust the process.

Christmas plans were being made and Cherie and Lyon were keen to have a big celebration now that their daughter was home. Though she'd never been very spoilt as their only child, Ruby was indeed much cherished by her parents and everyone at Peace Haven.

Mother and daughter sat at the dining table enjoying a cup of tea and discussing their plans for Christmas dinner.

'I think we could invite some of the clients we know who don't have any family. We always shut down for Christmas for about three weeks and we could invite those who have nowhere to go to,' said Cherie, knowing Ruby, too, had a heart for the lost and lonely.

'What a splendid idea— what about Belle and Milton? They might like to join us too.' Ruby asked.

'No, they can't come for Christmas dinner. They have their whole family arriving at their lodge, though I could mention it to them.'

'What about Annie and Murray?' Ruby was especially fond of Annie, a bond they formed early in her life.'

'Yes, they'll most likely join us. Their families are usually overseas or at their holiday homes at Christmas.'

It's strange, really. Everything has gone full circle here at Peace Haven.' Cherie passed Ruby another berry muffin.

'What do you mean?' Ruby looked baffled.

'I mean— how this communal retreat started off with the founders Belle and Milton who passed it on to Annie and Murray, and they passed it on to your father and I. Of course, each of us purchased the property from the other but we all remained as Trustees of the Peace Haven Trust. Belle and Milton have only resigned as directors in the last few years while Annie and Murray remain as directors. Perhaps you'll become a Director in the near future, Ruby.'

'I see what you mean by the full circle. I suppose I would complete it.'

'Well, if you marry a man who wants to join you in doing this work, it could turn out that way I suppose. It's too much for a single person to manage.' Her mother suddenly noticed Ruby going quiet, then said no more.'

'What groups have you coming this weekend?' asked Ruby, eager to get started and get her mind off disconcerting issues.

'Annie and Murray are going to be hosting some family who has lost their home in the floods in Pine Ridge. They've lost everything. There's also a couple who've had to walk off their farm on the Central Plateau due to the huge droughts they've had there the last few years. They have lost a lot of stock during the last two years and can't cope anymore. They've got a farm manager on their property while they have a break and decide what to do with the farm.'

'That's terrible, so stressful. It's good that Murray has had a lot of farming experience.'

'He understands, as he's had similar experiences on his own farm. He can help them get a government subsidy to help keep the farm going, but they may need to diversify with their farming business with the area being so prone to droughts.'

Ruby was impressed at the holistic service that Peace Haven offered to the community and she was proud of her parents. She could envisage being part of this for the rest of her life.

'Is there still significant domestic violence in this farming community after all these years?'

'I'm afraid so, Ruby—the climate has changed and the farms get the extremes of droughts, floods, and earthquakes. Livelihoods are affected, and they can't just abandon their land. Many women are isolated on huge farms miles from their neighbours and husbands often take the stress out on their wives, or turn to drink and sometimes finally to suicide.'

Ruby felt a chill run through her spine, being reminded of the story about her father's plight, though the situation was of a different nature.

'Ruby—I'd like you to think about attending this accreditation course for crisis intervention and grief counselling. It's only for six weeks part-time, and you'll be much more confident in a semi-counselling role if you do it. We've all completed it and it'll complement your Social Work Degree too, a good skill to have.'

'Okay, sure, I'll think about it and let you know. I've been thinking a lot lately of the vision I had for my life years ago. I always thought that one day I'd become a missionary in some remote overseas community like Kolkata, or Africa, living amongst the poor. But it never came to be. I suppose the work I did in Thailand with Rescue Net was missionary work.'

'You know, Ruby—these countries don't want people from the West setting themselves up as sanctimonious gurus taking over their lives. They want us to be practical—

training them to take care of themselves, showing them how it's done so their own people can teach them too. We need to equip them for life so they can cope and run their communities in a healthy way. So what you and the rest of us are doing to save those children is a mission in itself. Those who are rescued get trained and educated to help their own people and work amongst those who are in trouble.'

'I know what you're saying. I have thought along those lines myself and realise that this is what Peace Haven is about, here in our own community. It's a real ministry, a vital mission in our own country, especially with the high suicide rate. I can't wait to get right into it with your help, Mum.'

***

Christmas Day arrived and there was a delightful atmosphere at Peace Haven. Annie had been up early helping Cherie put the garlands of fresh, red poinsettias around the large lounge area and on the veranda. There was also an impressive array of other red flowers—rhododendrons, camellias, and roses with bunches of dark green holly between each stem of flowers to contrast.

The men got to work on ladders securing the colourful streamers that Cherie and Ruby had made, while Annie spent most of the day in the kitchen helping Chef create adventurous dishes with a Christmas theme.

Annie had shown Cherie how to bake a traditional Christmas cake with great success and they'd even managed to bake little fruit mince pies.

Lyon handed Cherie a clipboard. 'This is the list of guests who'd like to come for Christmas dinner. They've all accepted the invitation, except old Tom who's not well enough and Ernie is getting a visit from a niece for the first time in years.'

'Oh, poor Tom,' said Cherie. 'I think we could manage to take a little food parcel to him early in the morning which he can heat up. We can throw in some Christmas fruit pies too.'

Ruby was always impressed by the compassion her parents showed those who were struggling. Perhaps this is her destiny— to follow in their footsteps.

***

Christmas Eve was busy. Belle's son Harry had managed to bring Belle and her husband, Milton over for afternoon tea before their own tribe arrived at Seabird Lodge, much to Ruby's delight.

'Let's have a look at you, my dear.' The old matriarch took hold of Ruby's hand, gently pulling her towards her so she could see her more clearly.

'Well, well. You've certainly become a woman now, not the timid Ruby I once knew. I hear you've become a woman in your own right. Good for you!' Belle oozed years of wisdom and simple down-to-earth experience.

'I've heard so much about all your adventures overseas and your work with Rescue Net in Thailand. You're very brave. I think you've been doing God's work there.'

Ruby could see this old friend looked frail and had aged. She still had a copy of Belle's book written by a social worker about the matriarch's life—a research project at the university called Belle's Story.

'Lovely to see you again, Belle. I've missed you both, to be honest— but our work in Thailand is so worthwhile and vital.'

'Yes, I know, my dear, just like the work that's being done at Peace Haven too.'

Annie brought in a tiered cake plate full of fresh blueberry cupcakes with cream and mini savouries. Her friend, Amelia had taught her well before she had left Peace Haven.

'This feels like old times. I still feel at home here.' Belle slid down into the armchair, her old favourite.'

'I can't believe that this community has kept going for three generations, the snowball effect that Miriam my counsellor wrote about in her book. Any marriage prospects on the horizon Ruby? I hear there may be someone trying for your heart.'

Ruby tried not to show her indignation at this constant reminder of Julian, particularly since she still hadn't heard a word from him, as though he had dumped her. She almost burst into tears and quickly changed the subject. She just couldn't understand why she hadn't heard from him. Had she really been misled by him after all this time? Surely not.

When Belle and Milton went home, Ruby wandered out down the path toward the lake to have some quiet time by herself. She felt confused and tried to work out what it was that caused Julian to go into obscurity like this. She remembered he did this when he went back to England. That time, there was an explanation which he gave to Ruby when she arrived in England and he had sent her the air tickets. He was dealing with his mother's death and trying to help run the hotel with his brother. He wasn't in the right state of mind to put energy into a relationship temporarily. Perhaps he is feeling overwhelmed with work, Ruby said to herself, finding a way to relieve her inner tension, trying hard to ward off self-pity and tears.

***

Twenty-Eight

Cherie spotted Ruby taking herself off towards the lake by herself. She didn't run after her in case she wanted to be alone for a while. But she was out there a long time and Cherie decided to pick some flowers near the lake to check on her in case she needed a listening ear. Ruby looked up and saw her mother reaching up to prune a climbing rose.

'Mum, come on over and sit down for a while.'

Cherie was relieved her daughter still felt comfortable reaching out.

'I want to ask you something— it's confidential, so please keep it to yourself. Her mother noticed the sudden crevices in her forehead, a sign of emotional strain. She knew her daughter well.

'What is it, honey—is there anything wrong?'

'I ... I'm not so sure. It's Julian. I don't know where I'm at with him.'

'What do you mean—has something happened?'

'That's just it ... I don't know what's going on.' Cherie looked at the weight of disappointment on her daughter's face as Ruby sat wringing her hands—the corners of her usual upturned mouth slanted downwards as she stared at her feet.

'Remember what you told me about promises years ago? That there are false promises and rainbow promises. The rainbow promise is the one where there is actually hope and a future at the end of the rainbow, remember?'

'Yes, I did tell you that when you were very young. What did he promise you, Ruby?'

'He said he promised he would come and join me here at Peace Haven so we can build a ministry together for the lonely, lost, and broken-hearted. I haven't heard a thing from him since I left Bangkok, not one letter—not even a postcard!'

'I've known Julian a long time. You can trust him and you need to have faith that he'll come through for you. He wouldn't have made a false promise. He's not that kind of man. Just you wait and see.'

Ruby wished she had her mother's strong faith and the ability to trust and let go and let God.

***

On Christmas morning the sky was radiant. As Ruby woke, she was dazzled by the strong sunrays forcing their way through the crack in her curtains. She rose and stretched her long limbs like a new-born foal, dragging her curtains open to soak up the spectacular view of the sparkling lake in the distance. She was distracted by a chorus of birds perched in the tree next to her veranda. This is a taste of heaven, she thought. Then without warning, her mind drifted into sadness as she imagined Julian disappearing out of her life. She'd better pull herself together so that she doesn't spoil the day for everyone else.

'Hi everyone— you're all up early and on the ball,' she said, wandering into the dining room. 'What time are the guests arriving?' She tried to control the shaking in her hands as her edginess progressed.

'Your father has to go and pick up some of them in the van. I suppose they'll start arriving at about twelve and we'll have lunch around one. You could help put everything out on the table if you like, Ruby.' Her mother handed her some dishes with fruit mince pies.

Annie and Cherie were flat out helping Chef in the kitchen with the deserts while he mainly looked after the turkey and ham with all the trimmings.

As Ruby looked around the lounge which had been delightfully prepared for the guests, her mind wandered back to Rayong and the community there. What they would all be doing right now?

'Ruby! Cherie called from the kitchen. 'Would you mind going out to my herb garden by the hen house and pick some parsley for me?'

'Sure, how much do you need?'

'Just a handful for garnishing, thanks.'

As Ruby walked towards the hen house near the herb garden, one of the tame hens ran towards her, probably thinking she had some food. It followed her to the herb garden. As she bent down to pick the plants, she heard the van coming down the driveway and some commotion at the gate. She hurried back inside before the guests baled her up. She wanted to get dressed for lunch before they saw her.

She pulled out her navy-blue chenille skirt and white brocade blouse with elegant white court shoes to match. The perfect hostess. As she finished dressing, Cherie was knocking softly on her bedroom door.

'Are you in their Ruby? I need your help out here.'

'Yes, coming! I just need to change my clothes before guests start coming inside.'

She almost banged into her mother rushing out the door. 'Would you mind helping an elderly gentleman out of the van? Your father is busy escorting the others inside. His name is Charlie, and he's waiting for you to help him.'

'Okay, I'm off. Where are we taking them?'

'Straight into the lounge. We're serving tea and coffee first and the young Barbershop Singers have already arrived to perform once they are all seated.'

Even Ruby felt a sense of excited expectation with the planned events of the day and the loving communal atmosphere. She quickly wandered out to the van looking for Charlie, but there was no old man to be found. Perhaps he has already got out. 'Charlie, are you there?'

She wandered around to the back of the van. There in front of her, leaning on the back of the van next to a large suitcase was the outline of a younger man in a sports suit. She stood stunned ... is that ... no, it can't be.' The man turned around and Ruby nearly fell over with surprise and shook with sheer joy. 'Julian! What are you doing here? What a surprise!'

She ran into his arms, crying with relief as he squeezed the breath out of her.

'I wanted to wish you a happy Christmas in person, and I promised I would join you—remember?'

'Happy Christmas, Julian! Why didn't you write to me after I left? I thought you'd changed your mind.'

'I wanted to be sure that I could leave Rainbow Haven completely and not leave a mess or unfinished business so that you and I could look forward to a fresh start here at Peace Haven. I didn't want to muck you around.'

'How are the new staff settling in there?' Wait— let's go inside with the others, then perhaps we could go for a walk later to catch up.' Ruby lead him along the veranda to his room.

'I've moved into the flat with Mum and Dad. There are two bedrooms, so I have my own room.'

Julian dropped his suitcase in the guest room Cherie had prepared for him. Ruby showed him the ensuite where he could freshen up.

'The lounge is at the end of that hallway. I'll see you there soon. Come and join us all for coffee.'

She couldn't wait to tell Annie that Julian had arrived but she was still at her cottage with Murray.

'Ruby, you seem to be preoccupied. Can you help us with the morning tea?' Cherie winked at her daughter with a huge smile.

Ruby leaned over and whispered in her ear. 'You and Dad knew all along didn't you? How long did you know?'

'Oh, I think he and your father had planned it for some time so that he could surprise you on Christmas Day, but we were starting to worry about your emotional state when you didn't hear from him. I don't know if you could have endured it much longer, but you hung on to the promise, just as I reminded you.'

'Did Annie know too? She kept pressing me for information.'

'No—we decided not to tell anyone in case they inadvertently let it slip that he was coming and spoil his surprise. She'll be over with Murray soon.'

Ruby realised how hard it was to trust in a promise, but rainbow promises were different she was learning.

'Come on girl—let's bring this tea trolley in. I've already put the fruit mince pies out, but that will do for now, as they have a large Christmas lunch to eat yet.'

Julian appeared as charming and well-dressed as ever as he walked into the lounge for coffee. Cherie stood next to him. 'Julian, I'll do the rounds and introduce you. Folks— this is our new staff member Julian, who has just arrived all the way from a mission in Thailand.' Cherie was obviously satisfied that it was going to work well having Julian there otherwise she would have kept that quiet. He hadn't signed his contract yet.

Annie and Murray walked in to meet the guests before lunch. Annie came rushing up to Ruby. 'Well, girl, aren't you going to introduce me to your man?'

***

There was a joyful ambience and loving atmosphere at Peace Haven. Julian could see what Ruby meant when she told him about the transforming effect that this retreat had on people. The "walking wounded" is what they called their guests, who came there to recover from some kind of significant trauma or grief experience. He realised how he could be part of this too, and had a lot to offer them.

'Ruby—your father and I will clear up. Why don't you take Julian for a walk around the grounds and tell him a bit more about what we do here.'

Julian clasped Ruby's hand tight as they wandered along the shell path towards the lake where the dark red climbing roses on the white trellis were prolific. The wooden park benches had recently been whitewashed. Overhead were kowhai trees with bright yellow flowers. As they walked over the whitewashed, wooden bridge, a large golden carp fish jumped out of the water creating glistening ripples. It was a perfect, bright sunny day.

Ruby couldn't believe it—back home with the man of her dreams walking hand in hand on the property where she grew up when her mother was first widowed. Her life had gone full circle.

'I use to come here often when we moved here in my youth. Mum had married Dad and they purchased the lodge from Annie and Murray. When I needed space to sort my head out or meditate and pray, this is where I would come.'

Julian sensed there was a peaceful countenance over this particular spot that had a calming effect. He could understand what Ruby meant. There was something special about this place.

Ruby felt unusually relaxed in Julian's company, as though they'd been married for years, yet he still hadn't even proposed to her. They sat chatting on a park bench while a family of emerald green Muscovy ducks swam passed with their fluffy babies in tow.

'We'd better get back to help with lunch. We've got a house full, I think.' Ruby took Julian's hand which was given to her freely as they wandered back, half wanting to stay on the park bench together and savour the moment.

'We're going to be busy after Christmas. Peace Haven usually stays closed for about three weeks— at least it used to with the previous owners—especially Belle and Milton who had a large family staying for the Christmas holidays. But my parents do things a bit differently as they don't have a large family to consider. They believe this is the time that lonely, broken people need fellowship and joy in their lives. They only stay closed for a week.'

'What have they got in the pipeline?'

'Lyon wants to take you with him to meet some of the farmers in the area who are struggling, especially those whom he counsels. But he needs to speak to you about that. And Mum needs me to help in the local Women's Refuge for a day, where she usually works if there aren't many guests at Peace Haven. Annie and Murray use to look after the lodge while Mum was at the refuge.'

'Are there many bookings for the lodge when it re-opens?'

'We are fully booked except for the large family room. That's a room with another adjoining room and ensuite which we keep for emergency families from the refuge when it's full.'

'Come on, Cherry Pie, let's get back, and give them all a hand.'

Ruby could already see by his eagerness that Julian was going to fit in at Peace Haven. A perfect fit.

Chapter Twenty-Nine

The Christmas festivities together with the excitement of Julian's sudden arrival left Ruby overwhelmed. She looked forward to rearranging her room in the flat and getting ready for her training in crisis intervention the following week, which would give her another string to her bow in her life's work.

Julian accompanied Lyon to visit the farmers in crisis, as he needed to meet them personally seeing that he was going to be involved as a caseworker in their crisis intervention. Ruby would also be visiting the wives and children with her mother to see what support they required.

As the men drove back to Peace Haven past the lush, green hills surrounding Cromwell Mead, Lyon sounded Julian out. 'What do you think of all this so far? Do you think it will be something that will stir your heart? We need someone with your skills, so I hope you'll find it's what you're looking for.'

Julian was not a people-pleaser and equally not afraid to speak his mind. He had some questions in his head about the running of Peace Haven.

'I have a heart for the underdog, the oppressed, and the poor. I saw the rates for the rooms with ensuite and wondered how people who are struggling could afford the accommodation?'

'Most of the residents are subsidised by the government after referral by their Doctors, Social Workers, or psychologists. The Mental Health Foundation fund it. We receive a government subsidy for helping the farmers. There are plenty of Westerners in this country who are suffering—

ordinary people through no fault of their own just like those in the third world. We offer a service to the "walking wounded", through divorce, death, disability, fires, floods, and nervous burnout. That sort of thing. Then there are the lonely and lost ones. All these people need love and nurturing away from their own community where they won't be judged or pressured to conform. That's what we can offer at Peace Haven. That's how we are different from other retreats.

'I heard all about your philosophy from Ruby. It appears to be God-given and inspired. It's a great service which I'd like to be part of it. I'm interested in the crisis intervention training and doing part-time counselling, and perhaps learning to manage the lodge so Ruby and I can give you some relief.'

'Cherie and I were hoping you could eventually take it over from us—you, and Ruby, I mean. That's if this work suits you.'

'I don't see it as work. It's a ministry for us both.'

'Ha! That's what I was hoping you would say. It was a little test to see where you're at.' He chuckled.

Julian wasn't sure he liked the idea of being tested, but he realised Cherie and Lyon were also thinking about Ruby, and where this was all going.

'Lyon, I need to talk to you and Cherie about my intentions with Ruby. Can we do this tonight?'

'Sure, I'll let Cherie know when I get back. If you want privacy, I'll ask Cherie to speak with Annie and organise an excuse to send her over to Lavender Cottage after dinner. That way you'll be able to talk to us privately.'

'I appreciate that, thanks.' Julian bit down hard on his lip.

***

'Thanks for an awesome meal, Cherie. Did you cook this roast yourself?'

194

'Thanks. Yes, I did actually. Chef has the evening off. Ruby said you are partial to a traditional lamb roast dinner, being a conservative English gentleman.'

'I don't know about the gentleman business.' He grinned at Ruby revealing the dimple on his cheek that she found so cute.

'Yes, he is, he's the perfect gentleman.' She leaned over and kissed him.'

'Ruby—Annie asked if you wouldn't mind popping over to Lavender Cottage around seven to see her. She has a big wicker chest in her spare room full of linen and various treasures she wants you to go through. She's trying to get rid of stuff she's been storing for years,' said Cherie.

'Sure, that's okay, though I was going to drag out my old photos and show them to Julian tonight.'

Julian pulled a straight face. "Perhaps another night, Pie—your father has some business he wants to talk to me about ... you know, how things are done here at Peace Haven, amongst other things.'

'Oh alright if you insist. I know Annie was looking forward to a good old chin wag with me, so I'd better go over there.'

***

'Come and sit in the lounge, Julian. Would you like a cup of tea or coffee? I've Guinness if you'd rather.' Lyon was always the perfect host.

'No thanks, dinner was enough for me. Perhaps some water if you don't mind.'

'Cherie brought in a jug of spring water and glasses and placed them on the side-board then sat on the couch next to Julian. He sat squeezing his hands tight and shuffling his feet back and forth on the ground. Cherie jumped in to rescue him.

'It's so lovely to have you join us after all this time. We hope you'll be very happy here, Julian.'

'That's kind of you—the feeling's mutual. I was hoping to get the chance to talk to you both.' Perspiration dripped off the end of his nose. He quickly dragged a handkerchief out from his trouser pocket and wiped it.

'I haven't just come here to work at Peace Haven, I've come to be here with Ruby— you see, I love her and want to be with her … I mean forever.' He'd been holding his breath and took a gasp as silently as he could.

'That's marvellous, Julian, thanks so much for sharing this with us. We gathered that was high on the agenda,' said Cherie, giving him a warm smile.'

'The thing is, I want to ask Ruby to marry me, but I need your blessing.' He sat on the edge of his chair looking at them both intensely. Suddenly he coughed as though he was clearing a lump in his throat. He could hardly talk.

Cherie ran up and wrapped her arms around him, kissing him on the cheek. 'That's wonderful news, Julian! We were both hoping this would happen.'

'Good man.' Lyon shook his hand. 'I've worked alongside you and had plenty of good chats with you to convince me sufficiently that you're the real "salt of the earth". You're the right person for Ruby in my eyes. As long as she thinks so too you are almost there. You have our blessing.'

'I was hoping you could both help me tomorrow morning. I need to paint on an old sheet or something. I want to hang it up by the climbing roses near the lake. I'll propose to her on that.'

Cherie loved the romantic gesture and realised she would have to get Ruby off the property while they organise this.

'Tell you what. I'll take Ruby into town to buy a new dress and make an excuse that she needs suitable clothes for entertaining the guests.'

Julian could relax now, knowing he had the support of Ruby's parents. He could now confidently face her with the big question.

***

Ruby woke late. Her alarm had not gone off for some reason. She quickly showered and dressed.

'Sorry, Mum,' she muttered sleepily as she helped herself to her mother's home-made muesli and yoghurt. 'I slept in.'

'I want to take you to Maggie's Fashion store today to buy you a new dress—my treat. There are some gorgeous Poplin dresses in your favourite blues.'

'Really? That's sweet, Mum but honestly, you don't have to go to all that trouble. I can look after myself.'

'No, please Ruby—let me do this. I've been wanting to do it ever since you arrived home.'

'Okay, let's go. I must say I don't have many clothes except light dresses from Thailand. The rest are pretty worn out. Can I drive for a change?'

Julian and Murry had made a good job of the large flyer. Murray had found an old white groundsheet and red paint. Julian got to work with the paint-brush writing his message for Ruby.

'I don't think she could miss this one, mate. Where are you going to hang it?' asked Murray.

'On the trellis by the lake—the one with the roses. I'll need some nails and a hammer if you don't mind.'

'Come on, I'll help you to hang it up then you'd better go and get ready.'

Julian almost tripped on the doorsteps rushing into the house to wash up. He changed into a grey waist-coat, white shirt, and grey flannel trousers then looked in the mirror. When he heard the car coming down the driveway towards the lodge, he rushed out the back door taking the small bridle path down to the lake.

197

The plan was for Cherie to ask Ruby if she could walk down to the lake and pick some of the red roses to put in the guest rooms. She would see the flyer as she walked to the end of the path near the trellis. Julian would be waiting nearby.

Julian sat on the wooden bench by the lake trying to breathe normally, waiting for this plan to come to fruition.

***

'Ruby, I'll take your shopping bags inside and put them in your room if you could take these pruning shears and get a dozen of the dark red roses.'

Ruby didn't feel like going for a walk to the lake, as she was fatigued from all the excitement of the past week. Wandering around the shops all morning had made her weary, but she knew her mother couldn't do everything.

She set out on the little shell path towards the lake, wearing the beautiful spring dress her mother had just bought her. What was that? She thought she saw something red and white like a banner blowing around behind the kowhai tree. She strained her eyes to see but she was just out of range. She was mystified and stepped up her pace. As she rounded the corner past the camellia hedge, there it was, standing out like a ship's mast, boldly making a statement—

RUBY WILL YOU MARRY ME?

Ruby stopped dead in her track. Her heart missed a beat. *But where is he*?

'Well? What do you say young lady?'

Julian startled her kneeling on one knee.

'Will you do the honour of being my wife?' He called even louder to repeat it. Will you marry me?'

'Yes, I will, of course, I will!' Ruby called out as she walked along to rescue him from humbling himself too much. She chuckled to herself.

198

They embraced and kissed with passion this time, both relaxing in the knowledge that the mystery of love had become unveiled and they finally had made a commitment. The constant going back and forth in their relationship had come to an end. He produced a delicate silver ring with three dainty sapphires and tiny diamonds. Ruby's face beamed the whole time as they walked back hand in hand along the shell path. Her eyes remained glazed. The birds seemed to sing louder than before. The flowers smelled sweeter than ever. For Ruby, frozen for a moment in time, this was just a little taste of heaven.

Chapter Thirty

'How did it go?' Cherie started pulling on Ruby's arm, trying to control her sheer elation. 'What happened?'

'How did you know what Julian was up to?'

'Sorry, love—he spoke to your father yesterday then told me about it when you were visiting Annie at Lavender Cottage. He wanted to seek our blessing first and Murray helped him to make the banner. We were all in on it so it would be a surprise ... a pleasant one, I hope.'

'It was, Mum. It was amazing and so romantic. He is such a sweet guy, isn't he?'

'He sure is. You can't let this fish go. Let me see your ring.'

'It was his grandmother's—sapphires set in little diamonds. Isn't it gorgeous?' She stretched out her hand revealing her fine, slender fingers.

'It's gorgeous and it looks valuable too.'

'Apparently, he had kept it for years after his mother had given it to him for the girl he marries.'

'So—when is the big day— have you any plans?'

'We were hoping in a few months' time when the weather gets warmer then we can have a garden wedding. Mum, we were hoping we could have it here if you and Dad are in agreement.'

'I'm sure he'd love that. He'll be coming inside soon and you could talk to him. Where is Julian?'

'He rushed off to tell Murray how the proposal went as he'd gone to a lot of trouble to help Julian.'

'I was also wondering about who could marry us and remembered that Milton is a celebrant and married Annie and Murray here by the very spot where Julian proposed.

It's special out there by the lake. Do you think old Milton would be up to it?'

'Absolutely! He still goes for those long walks right around the bay each day. He's fit for his age and has all his faculties. He still mentors your father when needed. We could go out tomorrow and visit them with Julian then you can ask him yourself. I'm sure he'd be delighted. I'll phone them tonight. Lyon can hold the fort for us while we're out.'

Julian was busy with guests on the veranda— a couple who'd lost their home in the floods during the east coast cyclone. They'd suffered two onslaughts of the floods with insufficient time for recovery then lost everything, including their livestock on their small farm. Murray had been giving them support and Peace Haven provided temporary accommodation at a reduced rate until their house was built. It was almost finished, but the couple were still traumatised. The staff at Peace Haven offered practical support as well as mental and spiritual help, a holistic approach which included assistance to find work.

***

Ruby enjoyed the trip out to the coast to Shoal Bay where Milton and Belle lived. It brought back happy memories when they used to their families used to come together for the summer days.

'Julian—Mum and Dad are happy for us to have the reception in the lodge and have offered to pay for it as a wedding gift.'

'Is that right Cherie? That's pretty generous of you both. It sounds awesome. Thanks so much.' Julian leaned over the front passenger seat and stroked Ruby's neck affectionately, showing his approval.

'Wow, what an amazing view! No wonder they chose this place for their retirement. Seabird Lodge looks awesome.'

Unfamiliar with such beach locations in Devon with the beaches being so far away, Julian had seen nothing like this before.

As Cherie parked the car in the driveway, Belle waved from their balcony. She scurried inside and met her visitors at the front door with Milton in tow behind her. He put out his hand to greet Julian, and Belle wasted no time in giving him a welcome hug.

'Come on in, I have some coffee and fresh scones ready for you.' She hurried into the kitchen while Milton seated them in the lounge.

'Wowie! What an amazing view you have here.' Julian was already standing at the windows mesmerised.

'Yes, it is—One-hundred-and-eighty degree views all around. We never tire of it as there is always so much going on down on the water or at the beach front.'

'I can see what you mean. I wouldn't tire of a view like this for sure.' Julian walked over to the windows. 'But I wouldn't like to clean all this glass though.'

Belle brought in a trolley with fresh coffee next to a tiered plate of scones with strawberry jam and cream on one layer and mini home-made pastries on the other. On another tray stood a dated Queen Anne teapot covered in roses, under a cotton tea cosy that matched.

They sat chatting for a while and catching up with news about Rescue Net. Julian waited for the right moment then announced their engagement.

'The reason why we are here is to ask a special favour of you Milton. We are getting married in two months at Peace Haven and would like you to officiate. We heard you did such a good job at Annie and Murray's wedding. If you don't want to do it, we'll understand.

'Julian, I couldn't think of anything that would give me more pleasure than to do you that honour. It's a long while since I conducted a marriage ceremony. I'll look forward to it.'

'Of course, you're both invited, I mean to the reception as guests too', Ruby said quickly. 'It'll be like old times again for you all.'

'Why don't you send me a note in the mail confirming the date and details about the ceremony. I'll send you a list of all the information I need … better still, perhaps I'd better pay you both a visit soon and get all the documents and other information I need.'

'How about in a week's time? What about next Friday afternoon around two?'

'Great, that fits in with me. Before I come I'll drop off a list of questions in your letterbox, if you wouldn't mind completing it by Friday.'

'Thanks very much, Milton. We couldn't think of a more suitable person to conduct the ceremony.'

***

The two months went by a lot faster than Ruby had expected. After a day's work at the Women's Refuge, she was about to walk out to her car when a colleague called out, 'Something borrowed, something blue!'

Ruby hesitated on the top of the stairs and looked around.

'Here, I forgot to give you this clutch bag. It was my grandmother's, and she used it for her own wedding. If you don't think it's suitable, I won't mind.'

'Oh, Amie, it's gorgeous! That's French Chantilly lace and will go perfectly with my wedding dress. Are you sure?'

'I'm sure … I know you'll take good care of it and I want it to be used, especially by someone as nice as you are.'

Ruby felt really blessed by this friend she'd made in the short time she'd been back in Cromwell Mead. She felt honoured that she would trust her with something so precious.

'I hope you and your husband will be at the wedding. I don't know many people my own age in this area. A lot of my friends from university have all scattered.

'Of course, we will, I'll be looking forward to it. Please let me know if I can do anything.'

***

Back at Peace Haven, there was so much to organise. Cherie sank back in a chair rubbing her temples. She and Lyon had been up most of the night with a woman in crisis who was recently widowed and her farm was going to be put up for sale. Her adult children lived overseas and one of her sons was trying to organise the sale of the farm. She didn't want to leave it. Murray had become involved and suggested he could go out to the farm to talk to her son about some options which may enable her to keep the farm going with a manager.

'Don't worry, Cherie. Murray will handle it,' said Annie. 'You and Lyon just concentrate on getting your daughter married. I've got some of the women from the Country Women's Institute to help you with catering. There are a lot of men and women in the community who are grateful for the help they've received from you all at Peace Haven. It's your time to receive now.' Annie put an arm around her as though reassuring her it was okay to let go.'

***

The night before the wedding, Cherie sat on the veranda with Lyon, taking a break before the big day. She'd been running around with Annie all day, meeting up with some of the women helpers, organizing catering, flowers, and decorating the lodge.

204

Lyon carefully picked up the vintage china teapot to pour Cherie a second cup of tea.

'How's your leg feeling love? I noticed you were limping tonight. You need to get it up or get off it,' said Cherie.

'I haven't been on it too much. Murray and I have been organising some financial assistance for the woman who was going to lose her farm—you know, the widow whom we've been assisting. She's able to get aid from the Rural Assistance Hardship Fund for extreme hardship and employ a farm manager who'll diversify. It'll be a life changer for her. Her older son is coming back from overseas to help her. She's going to turn her huge farmhouse into a Bed and Breakfast for tourists and he'll help run it too.'

'Oh, I'm so relieved. I thought she'd lose the farm. She's still quite wobbly emotionally though, and Ruby and I have promised to support her by one of us visiting once a week. She's also going to come here to join the Women's Support Group each week until she gets back on her feet.

'That's great, Cherie, she'll really benefit from that.'

'I gave her a bit of my testimony and told her how my faith in Christ gave me the strength to carry on when I was suddenly widowed by a tragedy. She seemed to relate to me.'

'That just goes to show that our work here at Peace Haven is not in vain. We've all come from backgrounds of hardship or tragedy, and the people with whom we come in contact with this work can really relate and see us as being real.'

'Well, we'd better get some sleep for the big day ahead tomorrow. Ruby is already asleep—quite exhausted I think. Julian is staying at Lavender Cottage with Murray and Annie tonight and they'll keep him away until the ceremony.

***

The big day arrived. Ruby woke early after a peaceful night's sleep. The weather was perfect—not the slightest breeze. The sky was clear—the most intense blue she'd ever seen. Even the bellbirds seemed to sing louder and more joyful than usual.

'Come on— rise and shine. We have got a lot to do to get you looking like Guinevere today. Now off you go and have a good breakfast. When you've freshened up, Mrs Elder from Ambridge Farm is coming to do your hair.'

Normally, Ruby wouldn't allow her mother to fuss over her and treat her like a little girl, but just this once she thought she'd let it go and let her have her moment.

'Murray has been busy fussing over Julian, as though he was his son, so you need not worry about him. They're busy decorating the inside courtyard for the ceremony and reception. I think it best that we stay here. Ah, the door—it's Mrs Elder.'

****

Ruby looked a picture with her long soft ringlets with mini white chrysanthemums threaded throughout. Her soft, honey-coloured hair glistened in the morning sunshine as she sat on the veranda outside her bedroom. She sat alone with her pot of Earl Grey tea and one of Annie's blueberry muffins, taking the opportunity to meditate.

'God, my future is in your hands. I pray that you'll really bless our marriage and use us both in your service to help others to come to know your power, your love, and your way of life. Just like you did for Mum and Lyon and the rest of the folk here at Peace Haven.'

'Are you out there, Ruby?' Cherie called from down the passageway. 'It's time to get ready. You'd better start getting dressed. I'll help you.'

'Thanks, Mum, I'll need help alright. I'm so nervous I'll probably put that dress on back to front.'

Chapter Thirty-One

Ruby appeared as a princess in her wedding gown. The English Brocade dress tapered to reveal the subtle curves of her waist and hips. The shoes she had chosen—white satin and lace occasion shoes with little silver roses on the toes, showed off her petite shapely ankles. She looked through the window and saw Milton, the celebrant walking towards the lake and took an antacid tablet from her clutch bag and chewed on it.

Julian was already waiting for her in the garden by the lake where the ceremony was about to take place.

'Where are you, girl? I hope you haven't made a run for it,' said Lyon, poking his head through the veranda door. 'They are ready for you down there. Are you all set now?'

'Ready—can you walk down the path with me in case I buckle over? I'm so nervous my knees are knocking together.' Her father smiled. 'I am privileged to chaperone my daughter to the altar.'

The quartet of musicians, friends of Lyon's, were already seated and playing pieces that Ruby and Julian had already chosen.

As Ruby walked along the pathway, passing under the white, trellis archway covered in large red roses, the musicians began playing their special wedding song, "Love Changes Everything" with a male vocalist.

The setting was perfect and Julian stood agaze with Ruby's beauty this special day. He hadn't often taken particular notice of her looks as he was always captured by her heart and her soul. But today he was mesmerised.

***

The coloured fairy lights and tall, solar mock gas lamps illuminated the barn so brightly it could be seen from the main road. The music, though it was slow dance music, was loud but pleasant. The ensemble that had played for the wedding ceremony now had some additions, local chaps who put a professional finishing touch to this small band of skilled musicians.

Annie and Murray were in their element. The last time the barn was used for a big dance was for their own wedding. This brought back lots of memories. For Ruby, this was another dream come true. A big barn dance with all the locals and friends of Peace Haven.

The next day, many of the men and women from their local church came to clean up the hall. For them, this was an honour

***

The happy honeymooners returned from their holiday in the mountains to find some big changes ahead at Peace Haven. Cherie had welcomed them home with a special tea party and invited Annie and Murray to join them.

'We feel a bit guilty having to land this on you so soon when you've barely set foot inside the door—but we have to go to Thailand and help out at Rescue Net. They've got a raid planned for a brothel in Pattaya, and Rolando and Gamon need to urgently fly to Canada. Rolando's father has died.'

'Oh, really? Poor Rolando. He spoke highly of his father. At least he has a large extended family to help his mother.'

'We thought we would go on Friday. Phillipe can get us from the airport.' Lyon had his nose in his diary, tapping the book with his pen.

Annie and Murray were eager to say something.

'We thought you two might like to have some privacy while your folks are away and want to offer you Lavender

208

Cottage. We have arranged to say in the lodge in your parent's flat while they are away. What do you say?'

Ruby looked at Julian, knowing they both needed some time together adjusting to their new way of life. She whispered something to him and he nodded at Annie and Murray.

'Sounds wonderful—are you sure though ... I mean, it's your home you're giving up.'

'Well, it's only temporarily until they get back, then we'll see.'

'How long will you be away this time, Mum?

'Six months. Your father wants to help Phillipe train another new fellow for the raids and Gamon is expecting her baby next month. I thought I would help her get on her feet until the child is almost weaned. She doesn't have her own mother to support her so she'll need help.'

'That's so kind, Mum, you're a sweetie.' Ruby knew the devotion her mother had given to her as a young girl without a father and was delighted to have her share this compassion and generosity with others.

'God willing, all will go well and they'll still manage to run Rainbow Haven with Phillipe's help, and of course Isra's too. They have the nurse to call on if they get stuck. We're trying to foster the independence of the local people to manage these aid organisations themselves and not rely on overseas entities. It's healthier to encourage this. We're preparing them to completely take over the management of Rainbow Haven. That's why we need to spend some time there when Gamon and Rolando get back.

***

Annie and Murray were supportive in coming alongside Ruby and Julian. They even made sure they could handle the accounts.

It was the end of a long day. Ruby and Julian had just finished dealing with a stressed family who had lost their home in the recent floods. They sat on the veranda, a favourite place for them both at the end of the day. The fragrant Stephanotis was in full bloom and spread along the railing.

'What do you think of all this?' Ruby leaned on Julian's shoulder as he pulled her closer. A couple of tui birds sat above them in the overhanging Kowhai, making such a racket they almost drowned out their words.

'It's exactly as I envisaged when I knew God was leading me to join you after days of prayer and petitioning God. It's as though he gave me a vision of you and I running Peace Haven, but I needed to be sure, so didn't rush my decision to come straight away.'

'I think Mum and Dad are wanting to pull right back and let us manage it already. Annie and Murray are retired but still want to be involved in the running of the lodge and Murray plans to do part-time counselling too which will be a great help.'

'It's all working out just as I sensed it would. It's as though history has really repeated itself. We are following in my parent's footsteps, just as they have followed in Belle's and Milton's footsteps.'

'You mean like a circle of love. All links in a strong chain.'

Ruby looked out towards the lake, capturing a view of the weeping willows dancing in the evening breeze creating ripples on the still water.

'This reminds me of the times Belle and Milton used to sit on this cane couch, snuggled into each other. Mum would get me to take them a tray of muffins and tea at the end of the day. Mum and Dad followed suit and now we are doing it too. It has been a well-used couch for many a prayer and meditation in its time.'

'Perhaps in years to come our children will be doing the same.' Julian said, presumptuously—but this time Ruby didn't seem to mind, as she knew it was probably quite true.

'Are you two lovebirds ready for supper? I've made some of those fresh berry tarts you like, Ruby,' said Annie, who had just arrived in the doorway.

***

Spring came with a big welcome from Ruby who felt the winter always left her feeling drained and fatigued. The spring daffodils and freesias dominated the lodge, and she never wearied of the strong fragrance that emanated from them. Annie had been busy bustling in and out of each bedroom putting fresh flowers into the little vases on the bedside tables. The wooden birdhouse on a pole was busy with mother birds, mainly tui feeding their young with the sugar syrup and seeds that Annie put out each day. Ruby could just sit all day watching them, especially seeing the fat baby birds sitting there with their mouths wide open and the devoted mothers, usually skinny ones, doting over the plump babies. This was her favourite time of the year.

'Ruby, I've just come off the phone after talking to a fellow called Selby. He was a great success story many years ago here at Peace Haven. Murray, Belle, and Milton completely turned his life around, especially Murray,' said Annie. 'I have memories of when I first met Murray in those days too.

'Oh really—what happened to him?'

'Remember the book your mother wrote called "Belle's Story"? You read it didn't you? Selby's story of recovery was in that book too.'

'My goodness, it was too. I remember He lost his leg in a motorcycle accident and ended up doing an apprenticeship with Murray's friend.'

'That's right. He's now a qualified carpenter and farm labourer—married with a couple of children whom he wants to bring to see us. They've made a booking for this coming weekend.'

'What a pity Belle and Milton won't see them.' He is another one of Peace Haven's miracles.

'I must let Murray know, as Selby used to live with him before we married, and he hasn't seen him for years.' Annie put down the guest register as if in deep thought.

Ruby was also reminded of the healing her mother had experienced through Annie's input at that time. She realised what far-reaching benefits Peace Haven had been all these years and the way God had lead each one of them to bring about healing and restoration in the lives of others. Peace Haven was Cromwell Mead's best-kept secret and she was part of it.

'I'd like to see Murray's face as you tell him the news.'

'Of course ... why don't you pop over later and I'll wait until you come before I say anything. You can surprise him.'

Chapter Thirty-Two

'Come on in, Ruby I've just made tea and I have a few chocolate brownies left which I hid from Murray... no, just joking. I made them just for you.'

'I've got some great news for you both. Guess who made a booking for this weekend ... it's Selby and his family—remember him? He boarded with you for a while.'

Murray pulled his lazy-boy chair upright and passed the plate of brownies to Ruby.

'Selby, really? That's great. I haven't seen him for years. You say he has a family?'

Annie started pouring tea from her Wedgewood teapot, a special gift from Belle.

'He has two little girls and is still fully employed as a furniture maker and casual farm labourer.'

'We're all having dinner together on Saturday night, Murray. That'll be very special won't it?' Annie added.

'That's going to be interesting. It'll just be like old times. I'll look forward to that for sure.' Murray removed his reading glasses and started rubbing his eyes.

Ruby decided it was time to let them rest. She was exuberant that they were both about to receive a real blessing seeing Selby and his family. They'll really see some of the fruits of their labour.

She wandered back along the path behind the lodge, pulling out a few weeds on the way and met Julian on the steps scraping mud off his boots.

'I thought I'd better get them cleaned up before Annie sees them. She'll think I'll be walking the mud through the dining room she just vacuumed. Of course, I wouldn't— but the way she looked at me with my boots on when I walked on the veranda was enough to tell me to get cleaning!'

Ruby laughed. 'I'm so pleased she's training you well, Julian. Let's grab a cup of tea and bring it out here. The sunset is beautiful tonight and I feel like a chat. Hold on, I'll just run and grab my shawl to put around my shoulders. There's a bit of a breeze coming up.'

'It's an awesome evening though. Look at those hills. They look like an oil painting. The sky's an amazing colour—a palette of soft pastels. Anyway, what is it you wanted to chat about?'

'Nothing serious. Just a revelation that came to me today. I want to share it with you.'

'Of you go—I'm all ears.' He pulled her closer.

'It's strange how God works in mysterious ways. He can fulfil one's hopes and dreams in ways that we would never have expected.'

'What do you mean?'

'Well, ever since I was a young girl, in my early teens, I had this strong desire to be a missionary in some far off remote place like Africa or China. I used to read about women who would go to live in dangerous places—women like Jackie Pullinger who worked on the streets of Hong Kong amongst drug addicts and hardened criminals. Or like Irene Gleeson who lived in a caravan in war-torn Uganda. But the circumstances of my life kept standing in the way of me doing that.

When I really started thinking about it seriously, I didn't have the courage to go to such dangerous countries. I knew it had to be a divine calling or I would be too fearful and now it's too late.'

'So what is the revelation?' Julian asked, aware that Ruby often had trouble getting to the point.

'I've come to realise that I—or you and I are actually in a mission field already and have been in one for years. First in Thailand of course and especially here at Peace Haven. This is a very special mission field too. There are so many people hurting in our own community. Suffering comes in many forms, not just homelessness and poverty. You and I are missionaries, right where we are. God has shown me this.'

'I wondered how long it would take for you to say what has been on my mind for ages. God has also revealed this to me. In fact the first month I had arrived at Peace Haven, I realised that this was where God wanted us both.'

Ruby felt a strong sense of fulfilment. There really was a hope and a future as she had read in her Bible and had made sure to record it in her journal.

***

Back in Thailand, Cherie ran to the phone which Isra had passed her. 'Hi, Ruby, good to hear from you. Is everything okay? I'm sorry we've been away such a long time, but we need to get all the systems here functioning properly before we leave.'

'Mum, it's not what I'm ringing about. I've got some news for you ... good news. I'm going to have a baby.'

'What, really? That's marvellous! Congratulations. What does Julian think of it?' She started to cry with joy then Ruby heard her quickly stifle it.

'He's over the moon and can't stop telling everyone. He's so happy Mum.'

'When are you due? I'll definitely be there to support you.'

'I'm three months now. I didn't want to say anything until the scan. I had it yesterday and it's going to be a girl.'

'Wow! That's so amazing. At least we have plenty of time to get back home, but we'll be back long before that, as you'll

start to get tired towards the end. I'll so look forward to it
Ruby, it's wonderful news.'

***

'Life is full of swings and roundabouts, said Julian
struggling with his black tie as he was getting ready for
Milton's funeral.

'Here, let me help—you mean that we have a new life
coming and Belle has lost a life.' Ruby straightened his tie
and turned down his collar.

'Or when one door shuts, another opens.'

'Yes, I know. It's the same old irony of life which keeps
happening over and over.' Ruby's own life had been full of
swings and roundabouts.

'We'd better get going down to the chapel. Poor old Belle.
She and Milton had been together for a long time, although
they'd both been widowed and remarried later in life. She'll
miss him dearly.'

'She could come and stay here for a while, although her
son, Harry is running Seabird Lodge now and he and his
wife will look after her. She also has her other son, Jimmy,
and wife, Penny living close by too. She'll probably want to
stay close to them.'

The songs during the service were real tear jerkers. They
reminded Ruby and Cherie of the special features of Milton's
life.

Ruby became tearful as they sang a song she knew well,
"*Walk with God*", especially the line that went—

"*He will not fail me as long as my faith is strong,
whatever road I may walk alone.*"

The person most upset during the funeral service was
Murray, who momentarily removed himself from the church
when he realised his long friendship with this wonderful
caring man was at an end.

***

216

'Ah! Ow! I've got to get to the bathroom.' Ruby rolled onto her side trying to reach the night light. She staggered out of bed and bent over holding her abdomen. 'Ow! Julian! I think I might be in labour ... help me to the bathroom, please. Ah!'

'Don't you think we should get you to the birthing unit? I'll phone the midwife if you think you're in labour.'

'I think you'd better, I'm getting bad cramps. They must be contractions.'

Julian came off the phone and helped Ruby with the bag they had pre-packed ready for the big event when it happened. 'I'll let your Mum know before I bring the car around to the door.'

Cherie came rushing down the corridor, trying to calm Ruby down. 'Remember what you learned at the ante-natal class. Just start panting slowly, gently, and don't push.'

Lyon put his head through the door of the lounge, wondering what all the commotion was. 'Is there anything I can do?'

'Yes—please let Annie and Murray know that Ruby's time has come and Julian and I are off to the birthing unit. If we're there most of the night, they will have to manage the new guests arriving tomorrow.'

Julian parked right next to the front door-steps and bundled Ruby into the back of the car with Cherie. 'I'll try to drive as fast as I can as safely as possible.'

He arrived at the drop-off area in front of the emergency room, almost tripping over himself trying to get out of the car in a hurry. While Cherie helped Ruby out of the car between contractions, Julian rushed inside, running straight up to the first nurse he saw in the corridor. 'Quick, hurry, please! My wife needs a stretcher or something. Please help her!' The nurse appeared amused at this man's overreaction to a normal human process.

'Don't you worry, she'll be fine.' She put her arm around Ruby and helped her shuffle along the corridor. 'You come with me, sweetie and then I'll see where your midwife is. What is her name did you say? Until then, one of our team will take care of you. This is your room.'

Ruby stood doubled over again, groaning like a beached whale and eyeballed Julian.

'I thought you had already phoned Meg, Julian? Where is she?' Ruby frowned at him, not coping with the pain and oblivious to the fact that he had no control over the midwife.

Meg arrived about ten minutes later and examined Ruby to see how far she was.

'Not long now, my dear. Julian, you come and sit here and massage her back if she wants. It'll help her to relax. Here … I'll just show you how it's done first.'

'Thanks, Meg. I was shown at the ante-natal classes, but I've forgotten how to do it already.'

Cherie sat out in the day room, praying for a safe delivery for both mother and child.

'Please, Lord, give her the strength to cope with the pain.'

Ever since Ruby fell pregnant, Cherie had been praying that Ruby would keep good health and give birth to a strong healthy baby who would also become an ambassador for Christ.

It seemed to take forever and Cherie couldn't stop herself from continually putting her head through the door.

'Julian,' she whispered to him. 'Do you want a break? I can take over if you want to grab a cup of tea.'

'I will if you don't mind. I need the bathroom. I don't want to miss the big moment, so please get me if anything happens.'

Cherie sat next to the bed holding Ruby's hand while Meg kept Ruby focusing on her breathing.

'Come on, Ruby, one last big push now!'

Julian had just come back in the room to see his baby girl's black hair as her head appeared. Ruby breathed a sigh of relief as she heard a loud cry when the midwives cleaned her baby.

Julian was overcome with joy. He burst into tears as the midwife placed their new-born baby on Ruby's abdomen. Cherie was equally ecstatic but concentrated on helping her daughter hold the infant.

'Mum—we're calling her Georgie after Grandad.'

'I like that. What a lovely remembrance of him. He would have liked that too if he were still alive.

***

Lyon had been busy digging up potatoes in the extensive vegetable garden, ready for the traditional lamb roast Chef was preparing. Murray appeared, peering at the garden while sizing up the crop.

'Not bad for an amateur eh! What have you been feeding these with?'

'It's all that chook manure from those hens in your backyard. You must be feeding them well too. By the way— I need to talk to you about something important. Would you mind if we go somewhere private? Come on inside, I'll put the kettle on.'

'Sure, no problem. Cherie and Annie are busy inside with Ruby and baby Georgie, so I'm free for a chat.'

Murray, well-trained by Annie, took down the china teapot from the shelf and offered tea and started pouring. He placed Annie's fresh muffins onto a Royal Albert china plate and passed it to Lyon. Quite a contrast from the bachelor life Murray had lived before he had married Annie.

'Annie and I have been making a few plans for our retirement. Belle and her family have decided to sell off the half-acre of land next to Seabird Lodge, as they don't want the maintenance of it. They've given Annie and me the first option.'

'But what will you do with an empty piece of land at Shoal Bay?' Lyon asked, buttering another blueberry muffin.

'We're looking at moving a portable cottage on there—you know, like the ones you see on the main road coming into Cromwell Mead. They're not expensive, and if we buy the land, we can retire there.'

'What will I do without my live-in lawnmower?' Lyon responded, with a half-smile.

'I've given it some thought and prayed of course. I'd like to offer to remain care-taker of your grounds part-time. I may be a bit tied up while we're getting our new cottage sorted out, but after that, I'll be at your service again.'

'Wow! This is quite a change, but I'm sure you know what you're doing. We'd be grateful for whatever help you're offering. Julian is pretty enterprising though and enjoys being outdoors. We should all manage. Our new domestic staff have proved themselves to be invaluable. They only work half days, but provide the input of someone who works full hours. We're lucky to have them.'

'Yes, Annie told me about them. What are their names again?'

'We call them Pablo and Angel. Her real name is Angelique but she allows us to call her Angel because that's what she's like.'

'I hear Pastor Michael sent them over to you. They're refugees. Isn't that right?'

'Yes, they've had a hard time the last few years.

'Ruby will miss Annie, I guess, with their mutual history. Annie's been like an Aunt to her.'

'That's another subject I want to discuss.' Murray awkwardly nibbled away at his muffin, carefully choosing his words.

'Annie would like to offer help with childcare for Georgie and free up Ruby and Cherie to take care of the guests. She doesn't mind the drive from Shoal Bay to Peace Haven and she'll be in her element now that her own grandchildren live so far away.'

'That sounds feasible, but she'd have to approach Ruby and Cherie about that. They were concerned about how they'd manage the guests when it gets very busy so they may take her up on that.'

'So, what will you do with Lavender Cottage?'

'I was just coming to that. We thought perhaps that Julian and Ruby may like to rent or buy it at a reasonable price. They'll probably need their own space now, with a new baby.'

'They'll be thrilled. I know Julian has some money that they had set aside for a house someday.'

'Yes, I know … Ruby had mentioned it to Annie.' Murray topped up his teacup.

'Annie and I will talk to them both and see if they want to make an offer.'

Well, things won't be the same without you both living here—considering you've been part of Peace Haven all these years.'

'Remember, there's a time for every season, and now it's our turn to pull back and make room for others.'

One of the Barnvelder chooks ran in through the door causing a commotion as Murray rushed around chasing it out the door. Lyon was doubled over with laughter at the sight of this burly farmer being given the run around by a little hen which continually outwitted him.

'I'd better be getting back now, Murray. I'll leave you to it. Thanks for the tea and we'll talk again soon.'

***

'Come on Cherry Pie, let's go. We're going to be late if we don't get going now. I said we'll be there for lunch at twelve. Have you got Georgie's food for later?' Julian gently picked up the infant car seat with the baby and wandered out to the car.

'Yes, it's in the cooler bin. Hold on … I forgot to grab those brownies I made for them.'

Ruby and Julian hadn't seen Annie and Murray since the new cottage at Shoal Bay had been finished, and they were nicely surprised as their car peered over the ridge, looking down onto the property.

'Wow! It's awesome, all the work they've done in six months. They must have been going day and night to get it finished.' Ruby had her face to the window, straining to look down onto the cottage from the top of the long private road.

'You know what Murray's like— I don't think he knows how to retire. I knew he'd find plenty to do.' Julian checked his speed as they coasted down the hill, aware of their tiny passenger on board.

The white wooden cottage was surrounded by old-fashioned, lilac roses minus the white picket fence. Whitewashed, stone retaining walls with raised gardens full of pink hydrangeas enclosed the young lawn, and a terracotta paved pathway met them by the garage.

Annie waved to them from the wooden veranda, trying to remove her apron in a hurry.

'Murray, they're here!'

Murray lay stretched out in a lazy-boy chair when they arrived in the driveway. He quickly got to his feet as they got out of the car and peered through the front window.

'Aha! I can see that retirement suits Murray very well,' said Lyon, chuckling away to himself as they entered the home. I hope he doesn't get too used to it just yet.'

'We even have a small sea view from our front veranda—see.' Annie proudly showed them around.

'By the way—old Belle popped in to see our new home with Harry. It's amazing that we are neighbours. She's getting very frail now.'

Ruby doubted whether Belle would see another Christmas. It wouldn't be the same without her around anymore—not for any of the staff at Peace Haven.

***

There was a pink envelope sitting on the hall table for Ruby. She could see by the kangaroo on the stamp that it was from Kate as she wandered back outside to sit on a wooden bench under the kowhai tree.

This time it was a card. When she read it, her neck muscles tensed. Frustration overwhelmed her.

The pink card was a wedding invitation from Kate and Merv. Kate was pleading for her to come to their little church wedding in Bonalbo in a month. How was Ruby going to tell her it was not going to be possible with the lodge to run and all their responsibilities?

'Why are you looking so grim ... is it bad news?' Lyon saw Ruby sitting on the seat with her face resting in her cupped hands and the corners of her mouth turned down.

'It's Kate. She's sent Julian and me a wedding invitation. They're getting married next month and I can't get there, just as she couldn't afford to come to my wedding.'

Lyon sat next to her on the bench. 'Mmm, it's not the end of the world now, is it? Perhaps we can come up with a compromise.'

'What do you mean by a compromise?'

'Well, your mother and I were trying to think how we could remunerate you and Julian for all the hard work you've both done around here over the years. We'd

223

discussed paying for you and Julian to have a holiday in Australia. There are cheap flights later in the year and Georgie will be a toddler by then. Easier to take on a plane.'

'Oh Dad, that's would be awesome! Wait till I tell Julian. He's never been there before. He'll love it.' She stood up and wrapped her arms around him, holding back tears of joy.

***

Ruby placed the feed for the hens into the receptacles in the henhouse. They almost knocked her over as they headed for the pellets of cracked corn. She remembered the hen Annie had named "Woody-Wood Pecker" when she was a young girl. There were a couple of hens that were like that, always trying to pick at her when she walked into the henhouse. She missed not seeing Annie at Lavender Cottage.

'Ruby, where are you? I need you inside to give us a hand.' Ruby bumped into her mother calling her at the side of the house. 'We're full tonight and I need help in the dining room.'

'I thought you weren't taking any more groups.'

'I'm not, but these people had booked before we made that decision.' Cherie followed her through the front door.

'I wanted to say to you that the old man who lives two doors down from Ferndale Farm is lonely and has not been coping lately. All his children live overseas. He's always so grateful when we do anything for him. I wondered if you and I could pay him a visit when this group leaves.'

'Maybe we could take him some of your berry muffins. I think he'd like that.'

'We've also got to visit that woman on Crawford Farm near the village, the one whose husband is battling cancer. He's gone into hospital for some treatment and she needs

224

some support. I think she may be coming here for some respite while he's in the hospital for a few weeks.'

'Sure ... it'll have to be when we have a lull. Probably when the lodge is not so busy and Julian can mind Georgie.'

Julian locked up the lodge after the last guest had gone to their room and arrived at Lavender Cottage in time to join Ruby for a light supper and pot of tea before turning in. They sat out on their patio on this warm summer's night, starring at the stars that resembled bright glow worms. They reminisced about all the adventures they had experienced since they'd met. Ruby elaborated on how the wonderful concept of Peace Haven had evolved and Belle and Milton's vision of a holistic retreat had not only come to fruition but had gone full circle. The values and goals of this altruistic spiritual sanctuary were being continued on.

Julian stroked the back of Ruby's long willowy hair and rested his head on her shoulder. He closed his eyes.

'I'm really bushed.' He yawned and rested his head on her shoulder.

Ruby stretched out her legs like a cat. 'You do realise that what we are doing here at Peace Haven is much the same as the work we were doing at Rainbow Haven. We are still rescuing helpless people in distress and assisting them on the pathway to healing and wholeness— enabling them to live their lives to their full potential. It's a continuation of the healing ministry.'

Ruby seemed to have been summing up her life as though she was trying to put it into perspective on a spiritual plane.

'That's what Mum was trying to tell me that day when she had said that there's a mission field right here in Cromwell Mead. God can use us right where we are to help bring about transformation and restoration in people's lives.'

The next day as Ruby was walking back from the lake towards the lodge at dusk, she spotted her mother on the veranda watching her daughter walking with two-year-old Georgie. Time had flown by since she was born. Ruby waved out and Georgie mimicked her mother.

Cherie was reminded of the time she came to convalesce at Peace Haven when Ruby was only a few months old. She had often walked out to the lake with Ruby in the pram. She then walked back along the crushed shell path bordered with roses. She had often seen Belle sitting on the veranda waving at her from the old wicker couch.

Lyon joined Cherie on that same couch with the floral seat cushion. It had been in the same place on the veranda for decades, ever since Belle and Milton had originally purchased Peace Haven lodge.

'It has been quite a profound experience living in this community all these years. I can always sense Belle and Milton's presence here still. They had such a strong influence in each of our lives that it seems strange that they have both passed on, said Cherie pensively.'

'God has led us all here—a perfect plan of his to reach a hurting community although we have all supported each other too. One big family,' Lyon said, placing an arm around his wife's shoulders as she started shivering.

Was it the thought of time past or was she getting cold? The summer evening was drawing to a close as a cool breeze drifted across the lake and caught Cherie's breath.

'Hi, there! You two look cosy all cuddled up on the couch.' Ruby climbed onto the veranda and sat next to them. 'Where is everybody? The lodge is so quiet.'

'We had some cancellations and the woman who lost her home in the floods moved out this morning. Her son came to collect her and she'll live with him until her home is replaced.'

'Oh, that's good. It was starting to get her down, poor woman.'

'Did you enjoy your walk with Georgie earlier?' asked Cherie.

'Yes, it was so interesting watching her little face as she was fascinated by all the flowers and butterflies. It's like mini heaven out by the lake.'

'That's what Belle would say when she used to walk with me out there.'

'Mum ... I've got something to show you. A surprise.'

Ruby rummaged around in her maroon, quilted shoulder bag, and pulled out a book. 'It's finished, I can't believe it has finally been printed.'

'What? Your book! Well, that's great Ruby. Can I read it? I'd like a copy if you have a spare one.'

'Sure, of course. I had some extra copies printed. It's going to be in the local libraries soon and some bookstores.'

Cherie picked up the book. It had an attractive cover showing a large stone farmhouse with a small lake nearby. The cover was attractively designed with an array of flowers surrounding the house. The novel "Peace Haven Revisited" was a fictional novel based on the lives and adventures of the families who managed the holistic retreat.

'Oh, Ruby! Belle and Milton would love to have read this. Their memories live on in your book.'

'Well, I wanted to make sure that Georgie knows how wonderful this community has been. What an important part it has played, not only in her life but also in the lives of many people who were once lonely, lost, and broken-hearted just like you were when you first came here. Let's hope that she and her own family will be part of this circle of love too.'

'Ruby—without unshakable faith, you wouldn't be where you are now. That's why you are so courageous.'

Ruby looked into the face of her mother.

'I remember when I was a young girl and going through an anxious time—you told me that courage is fear that has said its prayers. And I never forgot.'

As Ruby wandered back to Lavender Cottage to put Georgie to bed, Cherie quietly thanked God for his divine providence in their lives and especially for using that which was meant for evil for good in so many of their lives—to bless, encourage and aid the healing of many who had been led to Peace Haven retreat.

She pondered the verse she'd read in her bible that morning—

"Instead of your shame there shall be a double portion;

Instead of dishonour, they shall rejoice in their lot; therefore, in their land, they shall possess a double portion; they shall have everlasting joy."

She had realised that God's grace had been truly at work in her life and all those who had passed through Peace Haven.

****The End****

VISIT ME

Website: https://www.patriciasnelling.com/

https://www.facebook.com/PatriciaSnellingAuthor